Crimes and Crystal Balls

Nola Robertson

Copyright © 2022 Nola Robertson

Published by Nola Robertson, 2022

All rights reserved. No part of this publication may be reproduced, stored in a retrieval system, or transmitted, in any form or by any means, without the prior written permission of the author.

This is a work of fiction. Names, characters, places, and incidents are either the product of the author's imagination or are used fictitiously, and any resemblance to actual persons living or dead, business establishments, events, or locales, is entirely coincidental.

ISBN: 978-1-953213-39-6

Also by Nola Robertson

A Cumberpatch Cove Mystery

Death and Doubloons
Sabers, Sails, and Murder
Cauldrons and Corpses
Pets, Paws, and Poisons
Paints and Poltergeists
Crimes and Crystal Balls

Hawkins Harbor Cozy Mysteries

Lattes and Larceny (Prequel)
Bodies, Brews, and Beaches
Volleyballs, Vanilla Crème, and Vendettas

CHAPTER ONE

"We need to hurry before everything is gone," my father Jonathan said, nudging his brother Max as he quickened his pace on the sidewalk ahead of my best friends Shawna, Jade, and me.

They'd been anxiously waiting for the end-of-business clearance sale at The Booty Bazaar, the town's antique shop, for over a week. Now that the day had finally arrived, they acted like two excited children on their way to a toy store. Only the toys they coveted were authentic pirate relics, specifically anything that belonged to Martin Cumberpatch, the not-so-famous pirate our town was named after.

Max already owned one of his sabers and had it mounted in a glass case aboard the *Buccaneers Delight*, the boat he used to give pirate tours during the spring and summer months.

"The place has only been open for an hour," I said. "I don't think it got cleaned out that quickly."

The shop had actually been closed since the previous owner, Hildie Simpkins, ended up going to jail for taking the life of a local businessman. Granted, the man was a lowlife and into quite a few shady things, but I didn't think he deserved to die, and not in the manner she'd chosen for him.

Nadine Carmichael, Cumberpatch Cove's resident fortune teller, was buying the building to relocate her business. Hilde's cousin Nathan Hansley, who resided in Portland, was overseeing the sale of the property on her behalf. I didn't know the exact details of their arrangement or whether she got to keep part of the proceeds, but he'd agreed to let Nadine handle selling the store's inventory.

Everything that hadn't been authenticated as an antique was being sold at a discounted price. Given Nadine's close friendship with Grams, my grandmother, I was sure the discount would extend to some of the pirate relics my relatives wanted to buy. I wouldn't be surprised if she'd set aside some pieces so my father and uncle could peruse them first.

I wasn't the avid shopper my family and friends were, but I'd come along hoping to find some unique items to sell at Mysterious Baubles, my family's shop, or stash away as future gifts.

Of the three of us, Jade possessed the most knowledge when it came to fashion. I'd be happy spending every day in comfortable sweats or jeans and a T-shirt. She never tired of trying to improve the business casual wardrobe I wore to work every chance she got. Though her determination was admirable, I didn't want to spend my days walking around the shop in a pair of two-inch heels similar to the black ones she'd chosen to accessorize the teal dress she was currently wearing.

Shawna wasn't quite as bad. Her unique style included adding streaks to her curly light brown hair. Until she'd met Nate, she randomly changed the color and purchased matching clothes every few months to suit her mood. Shawna wasn't known for staying in long-lasting relationships. She'd managed to keep her boyfriend and the same shade of blue in her hair, which happened to be his favorite color, a lot longer than Jade and I had predicted.

I occasionally glanced in Jonathan and Max's direction as my friends and I navigated past several tables covered with sets of china, old lamps, and other glass items. The males were around the same height, taller than me, and standing close to six feet. Max was the burlier of the two and had more hair in his beard than my father had on the top of his head. If he'd been dressed in one of the outfits he wore to work, he would've fit right in with the shelves displaying sabers, swords, and cutlasses.

Every time they stopped to ooh and awe at something they found interesting, they reminded me of Shawna when we were teenagers. Though, now that I thought about it, she hadn't outgrown the habit.

Jade had also noticed their behavior and chuckled. "It's a good thing Grams volunteered to cover at the shop; otherwise, we'd be supervising all three of them."

Besides being a close friend since childhood, she was also a co-worker. My mother Caroline and grandmother, whose name was Abigail, Abby to her close friends, and Grams to my friends and me, had stayed behind so we could shop. Though I was certain the main reason she'd wanted me to go along was so I could keep an eye on my male relatives. "You can thank my mother later," I said. "It was her idea to split the three of them up."

"Yeah, but you have to admit they are kind of adorable and fun to watch," Shawna said.

"Give it time, and I'll bet you change your mind," I said. I'd been on too many outings with my family to know that anything considered 'adorable and fun' eventually led to embarrassment and trouble.

"Let's see if we can find Nadine," Jade said, heading toward the back of the room.

Nadine's shop, Get a Glimpse, was several blocks away from Swashbuckler Blvd., the town's main street where The Booty Bazaar was located. Her business did very well, but the space she rented was small, and I couldn't blame her for wanting to purchase her own building.

She already had quite a following from the locals, and with the new location, along with the influx of tourists, she was guaranteed to do even better. Shawna was one of her regular customers and was excited about the move. Besides having a standing appointment at the beginning of each year to discuss her future, she occasionally popped in to make sure her fate, destiny, or whatever Shawna liked to call it, was still on track.

Now that her shop was only a few blocks away from the Cumberpatch Cove Cantina where she worked, she'd be able to visit Nadine more often.

A large portion of the town's population believed in the paranormal, my family included. I, on the other hand, had been a skeptic most of my life. Until recently, when I'd developed the ability to see ghosts, I wasn't willing to believe that supernatural beings existed unless I could see them for myself.

My talent wasn't hereditary, nor was it something I'd been born with. I'd gotten the so-called gift, which I'd first considered a curse, after being zapped by a spirit seeker. The magical oblong piece of wood had been a birthday present from my father. He was obsessed with anything associated with the supernatural and thought his only daughter should be too.

After surviving the blue tentacles of death, the enchanted spirals that came out of the seeker, bound me in a cocoon, and forced me into unconsciousness, I'd been visited by several spirits. Spirits who'd died from unnatural deaths and couldn't move on to the afterlife without my help.

I'd also learned my ability only worked when I touched something that belonged to the deceased and not necessarily someone who'd died from a recent death. Something I'd learned on two separate occasions. The first was Martin Cumberpatch when I'd accidentally released him from a witch's curse. The second was when I'd handled a possession belonging to the tenant who'd rented my apartment before me.

Thinking about Martin reminded me of the last time I'd visited The Booty Bazaar searching for an eye patch that belonged to his mate Pete. My experience with the centuries-old ghost taught me to be wary of my surroundings. Some things in the shop were old, and I knew nothing about their history. That's why I maintained a look-but-don't-touch attitude as I strolled through the store.

Even though the room was cluttered with furniture, cabinets, and shelves, Nadine had done a great job of cleaning the place and organizing the inventory. Besides sending out flyers to all her current customers, she'd gotten the other shop owners in the area to hand out copies to anyone visiting their businesses.

"There she is," I said. Nadine was standing behind a glass display case toward the back of the store, helping a customer decide on one of the shelf's items. Her usual work outfit consisted of a medium-sleeved blouse beneath a vest and a dark skirt covered with miniature gold stars and moons. Today, she was dressed in a casual pair of pants and a cotton button-down shirt with her long brown hair in a single braid in front of her left shoulder.

As soon as she saw my friends and me, she smiled and gave us a friendly wave.

We strolled in her direction and waited for her to finish what she was doing. "Good morning, everyone. I'm so glad you could make it."

"There's no way we'd miss it," I said, glancing over my shoulder at my relatives. "Dad and Max would've camped out on the sidewalk if Grams and my mother hadn't stopped them."

Nadine laughed. "That must've been an interesting conversation. I'm sorry I missed it."

I'd noticed red sold tags on several of the larger items. "It looks like you're doing pretty well."

"Things are selling fairly quickly, and with any luck, I'll be able to start renovations sooner than I'd expected."

"How are you holding up?" Shawna asked.

"Other than being exhausted, I'm fine." Nadine tucked some loose strands behind her ear and puffed out a breath. "I'll be glad when I'm all moved in."

"Knowing my mother, I'm sure you'll have plenty of help when the time comes," I said. Caroline Spencer was an experienced pro in what she liked to call the art of motivation. I liked to call it manipulation since she'd fine-tuned her techniques on my friends and me plenty of times throughout the years.

She was notorious for finding reasons why we needed to join the committee for every event the town hosted, which equated to a lot since the town council prided itself on coordinating attractions to draw in tourists.

Thank goodness, it wasn't something I needed to worry about. There weren't any upcoming festivities scheduled at the moment. The only major task I currently had on my calendar was helping Nadine move.

The bell above the door tinkled, and two middle-aged women entered the shop, their excited chatter briefly drawing everyone's attention. Right after that, a man I'd never met entered the room through the doorway leading to the rear of the building, carrying a cardboard box. After placing the box on a nearby shelf, he glanced in our direction and forced a less-than-friendly smile.

He had a medium height and build and was dressed semi-professionally in a navy-blue suit, less a coordinating tie. He'd slicked his dark hair away from his face with an excessive amount of gel, making the slope of his nose and angular cheekbones more prominent.

Nadine had given us a tour of the place shortly after getting the keys, so I knew there was a storeroom in the back filled with additional inventory. It explained the box the man was carrying.

"Is that the appraiser Hilde's cousin recommended?"

Shawna asked.

I didn't know much about Nathan or the kind of business he owned. Hildie had mentioned that he made pirate saber and sword replicas, which he'd given her to sell in her store. After learning that she also embellished the truth, I didn't know if Nathan actually crafted the weapons himself or paid someone to do it for him. My guess was the latter.

I'd learned from Grams that Nathan had volunteered one of his employees to come down for a few days to help the transition go smoothly. Shawna and Jade thought he was being thoughtful, but I was more skeptical than my friends. I figured his gesture was a way of keeping an eye on his portion of the sales.

"Uh-huh," Nadine said. "Nathan told me he was very knowledgeable about antiques and should be able to answer any questions my customers might have."

Cumberpatch had a local expert Nadine could've used, but he was on vacation and would be out of town for the next couple of weeks.

"Come on, I'll introduce you." She motioned us to follow her with the tip of her head.

The man had his back to us and was pulling items out of the box to fill empty spots on a shelf. "Aaron," Nadine said.

The man spun around as if she'd startled him. "Yes."

"I'd like you to meet my friends. This is Rylee, Jade, and Shawna." Nadine pointed at each of us as she said our names.

"Are you enjoying your stay in Cumberpatch?" I asked.

"It's a little quaint for my tastes, but it's not bad," Aaron said.

I understood that some people had difficulty adjusting to a smaller community if they'd spent their entire life in a big city like Portland. Even so, I still took offense when he scrunched his face as if he'd taken a bite out of something with a bitter taste.

Seeing Shawna cross her arms and glare at him must have been unsettling because he quickly added, "The few times I stayed at the inn overseeing the bluff was pleasant."

Our town was located along the coast of Maine. The view he mentioned was breathtaking. "Were you here to see family and friends?" I asked. Even though I'd spent my entire life in Cumberpatch, I didn't know everyone in town. Still, if Aaron had been here to visit someone, it was possible I knew them.

"Uh," Aaron stammered.

Shawna didn't give him a chance to finish. "If you don't like our town, then why agree to come back?" She disguised her sarcasm with an overly sweet tone.

The familiar glint in her green eyes was usually a precursor to asking a barrage of questions that would make an already uncomfortable situation worse, especially for Aaron. The man didn't seem particularly personable, but he was here to help Nadine. I'd never relocated a business, but it had to be stressful. The last thing Nadine needed was to have her expert get upset enough to walk out.

"You might change your mind if you come back for our pirate festival," Jade, the diplomat in our group, said.

Aaron raised a brow, seemingly uninterested in her suggestion.

"I'm sure you have a lot to do, and we've taken up enough of your time," I said, slipping my arm through Shawna's. "Haven't we?" I tugged when she refused to budge.

Aaron appeared relieved when he reached for the box and hurried toward another set of shelves.

"Excuse me," a man said from behind us.

He'd arrived shortly after we had, and I'd glimpsed him methodically moving around the shop as if searching for something specific. I guessed his age to be in the late thirties, possibly early forties. The pale tone of his skin and the shadows beneath his eyes suggested a lack of sleep. His clothes were high-end brands but in a disheveled state.

"Are you the owner?" he asked, leveling his dark gaze at Nadine.

"I am," she said, smiling. "How can I help you?"

He placed one of her sales flyers on the counter next to her. "Do you still have this dagger?" he asked in an irritated tone as he tapped the picture of a featured item.

"If it's still available, it would be on one of those shelves over there," Nadine said, then pointed toward another display case. "I can show you if you like."

"I already checked, and it's not there." The man frowned and rubbed the back of his neck.

"I'm sorry, then someone must have already purchased it," Nadine replied, maintaining a professional tone. "Can I help you find something else instead? There's a nice selection of other knives and swords."

"No, I'm only interested in this dagger." He groaned. "Can you at least tell me who bought it?"

Nadine took a calming breath. "I'm afraid I can't do that. Most of the items were paid for with cash, and if someone used a credit card, I can't give out that information."

"Can't or won't?" The man leaned closer, his stance and voice meant to intimidate.

Like my friends and me, Nadine was used to handling emotional people. She clasped her hands together and, in a calming voice, said, "Both, I'm afraid." Noticing that they'd gained the attention of several other customers, she politely added, "Maybe you should leave."

I was prepared to help if the man didn't heed her advice and wanted to escalate the situation. By the concerned expressions on my friends' faces, they were also ready to step in. Aaron had taken his box and disappeared, most likely to another area of the shop. I could've relied on my father and uncle to intervene, but they were nowhere in sight.

After a long, dread-filled moment, the man took a step

back, then said, "Fine, I'm going," before heading toward the door.

"I guess he really wanted that dagger," Shawna said.

"I agree and wish he'd told us why he was making such a fuss," I said, my gaze fixed on the door after the man had exited. I didn't know about the others, but I was worried about the man's emotional state and wanted to ensure he wasn't coming back.

Nadine shuddered and said, "I sensed a darkness surrounding him. Maybe I should've offered to give him a reading." She wrinkled her nose. "Though I'm not sure it would've helped."

Before I was able to see ghosts and learned that witches existed, I would've scoffed at Nadine's comment. I might not have fortune-telling abilities, but I could sense that something was off with the man. I didn't think it had anything to do with visions of his future. "Was the dagger he wanted worth anything?" I asked.

"It's possible, but I've handled so many items already, I couldn't say for sure," Nadine said. "I had Aaron authenticate everything that looked valuable and had him record the information into a spreadsheet in my office. I thought the ornate design on the dagger's handle was impressive and would attract customers. It's the reason I included its picture on the flyer."

"On the upside, the flyers you posted seem to be working," Jade said.

"Seems like it, doesn't it?" Nadine chuckled. "Now, is there anything I can help you find?" She swept her hand through the air. "Or did Caroline send you along to keep Jonathan and Max out of trouble?"

Nadine knew my family well. I snorted, remembering my mother's comment about having fun but not to let my male relatives out of my sight, a task I'd already failed to do.

"Shawna and I came to shop," Jade said. "I'm pretty sure Rylee's the one who got stuck with babysitting duty."

"Nadine," a woman called from across the room. "Can you help us?"

"I'll be right there," Nadine said. "Everything needs to go, so if you girls find something you like and you're in the mood to haggle, please let me know." She winked, then set off to help the woman.

Now that Jade had mentioned babysitting, I figured it might be a good time to get a visual on my father and uncle. There were quite a few tall pieces of furniture in the middle of the room, which could easily hide them from view.

"Um, Rylee." A tap on my shoulder from Ben Hoopler kept me from searching for them.

Ben was in his early twenties and employed by the town's pirate museum. He'd agreed to work for Nadine part-time. His main job was assisting customers and bagging and boxing up items. He was also responsible for arranging local deliveries for items too large for customers to transport themselves. He'd rolled the cuffs of his shirt halfway up his forearms as if he expected to do a lot of hard work.

"Yeah," I said.

Ben nervously wrung his hands together. "Do you suppose you could ask your father and uncle to stop their sword fight before someone gets hurt?"

"You've got to be kidding," I muttered, shooting Shawna an I-told-you-so look. "Where are they?"

Ben hitched a thumb over his shoulder. "On the other side of those armoires over there."

"I'll take care of it," I said and hurried across the room. I glimpsed a flash of something shiny and heard metal clashing as I cautiously stepped through a gap between two book shelves.

Jonathan and Max had found a small area not filled with furniture and shelves and were swiping at each other with practiced ease. Their noises started drawing attention, increasing my concerns about someone getting hurt.

Telling them to stop wouldn't work. They'd just ignore me. Threatening them with a call to Grams had potential, but I was afraid once my eccentric grandmother arrived, she'd pick up a saber and join them.

Short of a fire breaking out, the appearance of something paranormal was the only thing that might draw their attention. I preferred telling the truth over fabricating information, but I figured a small embellishment wouldn't hurt if it saved lives and prevented injuries.

I walked over to the closest display case, raised my voice so I'd be heard over the repeated sword clanks, and said, "Oh, look, I found a book on casting spells."

Since my father and uncle were fascinated with anything related to my abilities, I tapped the glass and added, "Oooh, and there's one of those cool-looking pentagrams on the cover, and I think it's glowing."

As I'd hoped, my father and uncle assumed I'd found something magical and stopped swiping at each other, then rushed over to join my friends and me.

"Where?" my father said, squinting at the contents inside the display. "I don't see a book."

Shawna hadn't caught on to what I was doing and leaned in next to my father. "Me either."

"My mistake," I said, trying to hide my grin.

Even with her hand clamped over her mouth, Jade couldn't stifle her giggles.

My father finally realized what I'd done and frowned. "Rylee, that wasn't funny."

"Neither is having a sword fight in a store full of people." I held my hand out and wiggled my fingers until he handed me his weapon. Max was a little more reluctant, but he finally turned his over. "If I were you, I'd get back to shopping before all the things you wanted are gone. Jade and I need to get back to cover the store for mom and Grams." I left out the part where I also had to get ready for my date with Logan later. Though, if they continued to misbehave, I wasn't above reminding them that the town's handsome detective might frown on their adolescent behavior.

Max and my father stared at me as if they were waiting for something magical to happen. "Anything?" my father asked.

When his gaze shifted from my face to the sword, I wondered if the mock fight had been a ploy to get me to touch the antiques in order to resurrect a spirit. It wouldn't be the first time a family member or friend had used a similar tactic.

Luckily, I hadn't felt the slightest electrical tingle—a precursor to a ghostly appearance. I handed the weapons back to my relatives. "If we weren't related, I'd seriously consider popping down to the Classic Broom and buying a transformation potion from the Haverston sisters."

I didn't think the potion worked, but they did, so I wasn't surprised when both males paled and quickly disappeared to another part of the shop.

"How adamant are you on the being related thing?" Shawna asked. "Because if there's room for negotiation, I'll buy the potion for you."

"Maybe another time." I laughed even though I knew she was serious. For reasons I didn't understand, my friend was obsessed with transformation magic. When we were younger, Jade and I had talked her out of testing the theory on an ex-boyfriend after she'd gone through a bad breakup.

"Come on," Jade said, draping her arm over my shoulder. "Let's go check out the sales before *your* relatives cause any more trouble."

CHAPTER TWO

So far, my date with Logan had been quite enjoyable. Since my apartment was above my family's shop, Logan had parked his truck behind the building, and we'd walked to the Cumberpatch Cove Cantina for dinner.

Shawna had worked the day shift at the restaurant for years. I hadn't expected to run into her during our date. She hadn't mentioned her plans for the evening, but I assumed she'd be hanging out with Jade in their apartment or spending time with her boyfriend, Nate.

By the time we headed back to my place, where we planned to cuddle up on the couch for a few hours and watch a movie, the evening had descended into darkness. The occasional lamppost provided us with enough light to see where we were going, so stumbling on a crack in the sidewalk wasn't a problem.

Pedestrian traffic running along the storefronts was sparse, as were the vehicles traveling the street. Though the weather's transition between spring and summer was moving at a moderate pace, the night air still held a brisk chill. When I shivered and pulled the collar of my jacket closer to my neck, Logan wrapped his arm around my shoulder and tucked me against his side. "Better?"

"Much," I said, snuggling into his warmth as we walked at a comfortable pace.

"I'm just curious," he said after we'd crossed the street to the next block. "Have you given any more thought to what you're going to do once you're certified to be a spirit sleuther?"

When I'd first learned about my gift, I'd done everything possible to find out how to get rid of it. It had taken some time to accept that it wasn't going away, and I needed to adjust my life to accommodate future ghostly visits.

Spirits showing up wasn't an everyday occurrence, but it did seem to happen frequently. My job was to help them find their way to the afterlife. It was either that or end up being haunted forever. The task would be easier if all I had to do was find missing items or pass on a message to a loved one. Unfortunately, all the spirits I dealt with were victims of a crime.

Only a handful of people knew about my abilities, which included Logan. Being a police detective who was expected to uphold the law made things difficult and sometimes strained our relationship. So far, he'd been assigned to all the cases in town that involved a suspicious death, which were also linked to my unlucky ghosts.

Every ghostly encounter I'd had was the result of someone being murdered. Finding the killer drew my friends and me into dangerous situations. Situations we weren't necessarily equipped to deal with and sometimes required us to step outside the confines of the law.

I'd been lucky that every adventure we'd muddled through had a good outcome, and no one I cared about had gotten hurt. So far, any pleading I'd done to encourage Shawna and Jade to let me investigate alone hadn't worked. Even Grams interjected her assistance whether I wanted her to or not.

Shawna found a website during a trip we'd taken with Jade to Waxford Bay, so Barley could participate in a pet expo costume contest. She'd discovered Parasleuth, Inc., an organization that offered a program designed for my specific talent. Because my friends could be persuasive, especially when they combined their efforts, they'd spent a lot of time trying to convince me to sign up for the training.

If helping a new spirit move on to their afterlife didn't involve a time constraint, I would've been glad to wait for local law enforcement to solve the crimes. Fearing for everyone's safety and the possibility of missing a deadline made me agree with my friends and do additional research.

Jade's brother Bryce knew I was worried the certification might be a scam. Via his connections with people he trusted in the paranormal world, he'd discovered the organization had a stellar reputation and a lot of experience dealing with the supernatural.

Logan had voiced concerns about my safety and getting involved in his cases long before he'd learned about my abilities. He supported my efforts for improvement.

"I'm not certified yet," I said. "I'm still waiting to hear back on my application." I was worried I wouldn't pass the initial vetting process, that obtaining the much-needed training might never happen. Mainly because I hadn't received any notification from the online inquiry I'd submitted. The website information said applications could take up to six weeks to process, and only five weeks had passed.

As much as I wanted to be accepted, a part of me worried about what would happen if Parasleuth enrolled me in their program. I'd spent the majority of my life scoffing at the existence of anything paranormal, so learning the unknown existed had been unsettling. If I underwent training, would I discover I could do more than talk to ghosts and see magical auras?

During my last ghostly adventure, I'd learned that certain plants and potions, when combined with magic, created a signature essence when they came in contact with people or objects. For some reason, I could see the colorful residue left behind.

I inhaled a calming breath, refusing to let my stress get the better of me. "If I find out that mastering ghost sleuthing skills is the same as attending a military boot camp, I'll probably forgo signing up."

"I'm sure it won't be that bad." Logan chuckled.

"Maybe not, but there's always the chance my application will be rejected," I said.

"I don't have any connections in the supernatural world, but I have contacts in law enforcement. I'd be happy to make some calls or pull some strings to see if I can help you get into the program."

Surprised, I stopped in the middle of the sidewalk to face him. Logan was a follow-the-rules kind of guy. For him to make that type of offer was a big deal. "You'd really do that for me?"

Caring flickered in eyes the color of a dark whiskey. "Of course." He cupped my cheek, his hand warming my cold skin.

"Why?" I asked. Unless dealing with a ghost caused problems when it coincided with one of his cases, I thought we did a good job separating our personal and professional lives. Not only would getting certified give me the training I needed, but it would also change some aspects of my life. Aspects that would be challenging and require compromises that worked for both of us.

"When I'm working a case, I can't help you in an official capacity or allow you to actively be involved," Logan said. "I also know that telling you not to investigate and let me handle finding the killer won't do any good."

Before I could remind him why I kept interfering, he placed a finger to my lips. "I haven't forgotten about the afterlife deadline." He paused a moment, then said, "I have a feeling there might be more to your abilities than you've already discovered."

It was almost as if he'd read my recent thoughts. "Are

you sure you don't have some hidden supernatural skills of your own? Besides being a darned good detective, I mean."

"Not that I'm aware of," he said and winked. "I thought it would be nice to know if you had any additional skills you can use to protect yourself if the need arises."

Logan had an open mind, but he'd been like me. Things didn't exist unless you could see and hear them. His view had changed after he'd been drawn into my world and started having regular chats with Bryce and my father. Not only was Bryce a resident paranormal expert, but he was also the head of the Supernatural Spoof Squashers or spoofers for short.

"Like stunning someone by shooting balls of light from my hands," I teased.

"That would be amazing." He grinned and slipped his arms around my waist. "You haven't been holding out on me, have you?"

"Sorry, but no." I leaned into him, pressing my palms against the tan leather jacket covering his chest. Since he was taller than me, I had to tilt my head back to see his face. "I'll have to fight off the bad guys the old-fashioned way."

"As long as you promise me you'll be careful and call me before you run into trouble," he said.

"I'll do my best," I said. Since I never knew where searching for clues would take me or what I'd find when I got there, I couldn't promise to call ahead of time.

Logan pulled me closer. "I like having you around and don't want anything to happen to you."

"I see," I said, smiling. "I like you too and don't want anything to happen to me either."

"Great," he said, pressing a kiss to the top of my head, then taking my hand. "Now that we have that issue resolved, what do you say about stopping by Mattie's and grabbing some dessert before heading back to your place?"

I loved that Logan had a sweet tooth that matched mine. Mattie was my grandmother's best friend, and her coffee shop was across the street from my family's place. Besides having a convenient location, she made the best desserts in town. "Are you thinking about something with chocolate, caramel, or both?" I asked.

"Definitely both," he said, checking the street for traffic before leading me to the next block.

When we neared the front of The Booty Bazaar, or rather Get a Glimpse, once the remodeling was finished, I noticed the inside lights were off, but the front door was ajar. One of the glass panes was broken, and shards littered the sidewalk and interior entryway. "Logan," I said, the muscles in my chest tightening with the next few cautious steps.

"I see it," he said, his voice deepened as he pulled me to a stop. It always amazed me how quickly he could shift from a caring boyfriend into an unemotional detective. "I'm going inside to check around and need you to wait out here." He released my hand and moved toward the door.

Suddenly, the shadows seemed more prominent, scary even. I wasn't someone who usually cowered in fear, and if there'd been other people walking around, I might have been inclined to follow his instructions. I was also worried about Logan's safety. What if whoever had damaged the door was still in the shop? Would they lash out if they thought he was a threat? I figured the risk might be lower if I went with him. "No way," I said, latching onto his coat sleeve.

After giving me one of his intense glares, which would have had anyone else complying, he groaned. "Fine, but I want you to stay behind me." He retrieved a small flashlight from his coat pocket, then clicked on the light.

Any other time I might ask him what other items he kept in his pocket for emergency detecting. Since things had turned serious, I was more worried about what we'd find inside and decided to save the teasing for another time.

Nadine came to mind, and I rationalized my concern for her welfare by telling myself that the lights would still be on if she'd decided to work late. The dread skittering along my spine worsened as soon as we entered the store. There was no way to avoid the broken glass, and hearing it crackle beneath our footsteps didn't help my anxiety. The place was quiet, and I hoped whoever had broken into the store had already left.

"Do you think we're dealing with a professional?" I whispered. Thefts, at least in the businesses on Swashbuckler Blvd., rarely happened, if ever. The shops, my family's included, had never acquired a need for fancy security systems. I didn't think Nadine had recently installed one either, which would explain why no one from law enforcement had shown up yet.

"Experienced thieves don't usually break in where someone can see them," Logan said. "They would've entered through the back. It's most likely vandalism and done by local teenagers."

I took Logan at his word since he'd worked on the police force in Bangor before moving here. Coming from the larger city, he'd probably seen the aftermath of many different crimes. Over the last few months, I'd accidentally stumbled across a body on three occasions. It didn't make me an expert, nor was it something I wanted to do regularly, and I found myself hoping that this wasn't going to be the fourth.

I'd be okay if I never had to see another corpse again. As much as I disagreed with Jade and Shawna's assessment that I was now a murder magnet, there were times when I thought they might be right.

Logan aimed his flashlight to the left, found the main lighting panel, carefully flipped the switch, and filled the room with light.

"It looks like whoever broke in has already gone," I said, releasing my grip on his jacket. I wanted Logan to find the person responsible but was relieved to see that the place was empty. It was hard to know how a person would react when caught performing a criminal act or if they'd retaliate with force.

"Unless they're hiding in back," Logan said, clicking off his flashlight and returning it to his coat pocket. "Stay here while I take a look." He flipped another switch and disappeared into the lighted hallway, only to return a few minutes later.

"Anything?" I asked.

He shook his head. "You were here earlier. Can you tell if anything looks out of place?"

Logan had been working all day, so he hadn't gotten a chance to stop by. I took a step to the side and scanned the store's interior. None of the items on top of the table or on the nearby shelves had been disturbed.

Nadine kept the sliding glass doors locked on the cases containing the valuables she'd had authenticated. A few antiques were sitting on the shelves, but none of the cases appeared to be damaged.

Most of the bigger pieces of furniture were still sitting where I'd seen them earlier. Many shelves had an item here and there, and a few were completely empty. "It looks like quite a few things are gone, but Nadine could've sold them," I said.

I glanced toward the shelves where she kept a collection of antique weaponry. My gaze froze when I noticed a pair of men's loafers, sole side up, peeking out from behind the end of a nearby display case. I remembered a similar situation that happened before Halloween and experienced a deja vu moment. "I can say for certain that those men's shoes weren't there before." Or the feet and ankles covered by a thin pair of dark socks.

"Be careful not to touch anything," Logan said as he took my hand and led me closer.

I'd been right about it being a man. He was sprawled facedown on the floor, his hands outstretched on both sides as if he'd tried to prevent the fall and failed. A flashlight was lying to the side, the beam partially hidden beneath a nearby shelf. It looked like it might have rolled from his hand after he'd landed on the floor.

I didn't want to believe he was dead, but the blood-soaked fabric and dagger sticking out of his back made it impossible.

The light gray business jacket and dark pants he wore seemed familiar. It wasn't until I saw his pale face that I realized we'd met before. "I recognize this guy." I waved my shaking hand in his direction.

"From where?" Logan asked.

"He was in the store earlier and got into an argument with Nadine." One of her flyers was lying on the floor not far from him, providing proof of their altercation.

He hadn't been killed with the dagger he'd been asking about. The hilt protruding from his back didn't have the same elaborate design.

Logan turned to give me his full attention. "What kind of argument?"

"Wait." I took a step back and glared at him, knowing where his detective mind was going with the question. "You don't think Nadine did this, do you?"

"Rylee, you know how a murder investigation works, that everyone is a suspect until I can rule them out."

I did know how things worked, but it didn't stop me from wanting to defend Nadine and make sure she didn't get blamed for something she wasn't capable of doing. I might not have the same close relationship that Grams shared with her, but as far as I was concerned, she was like family.

When I refused to stop frowning, he sighed and ran his hand through the short dark strands on the side of his head. "Would it make you feel any better if I called Nadine after I report this to the station?" Logan asked in a softened tone which helped ease some of the irritation pulsing through my body.

I acknowledged that he was trying to accommodate his

role as my boyfriend without crossing any lines while doing his job. "Maybe," I said, willing to compromise.

After pulling out his cell, he contacted the station and provided them with brief details of what we'd found.

"I don't suppose you have Nadine's personal number, do you?" Logan asked.

"I do," I said, reaching into my purse and pulling out my cell. After several swipes and a few taps, I held up the screen so he could see the information.

"Nadine, this is Detective Prescott," Logan said, his voice deep, his tone professional again. "Would you mind coming down to your new shop?" He paused to listen to her response. "Yes, as soon as possible." Another pause. "We have a situation I'd rather not discuss over the phone."

CHAPTER THREE

Even though Swashbuckler Boulevard was the town's main street and the buildings were filled with businesses, there were residential neighborhoods a few blocks over. With the lights flashing on the police cruiser parked sideways on the street in front of the building, it wouldn't be long before a crowd of curious locals started gathering.

Logan asked Elliott Barnes, one of the police officers who'd arrived after he'd made his call to the station, to cordon off the sidewalk with yellow crime scene tape. I'd been politely asked to wait near the front door and out of the way. I knew Logan's reminder not to touch anything was the standard spiel the police gave at every crime scene, but I wondered if it was his way of keeping me from summoning the dead guy's spirit.

No ghost meant I wouldn't have a reason to get involved in another one of his cases. Not that I minded…much. Life was simpler without the added pressure of helping someone's spirit find their afterlife. Though I didn't want to admit it to Logan, or anyone else, there was a part of me who enjoyed sleuthing and the exhilaration that came from solving a mystery.

Shortly after Logan contacted Nadine, she'd arrived

with Grams. My grandmother leaned toward the eccentric side and got into trouble regularly. But she supported her friends and refused to leave Nadine's side, ignoring Logan when he'd insisted she wait with me.

Grams must've been home, possibly in bed, when Nadine called her. Her short dark strands, heavily peppered with silver, were mussed. She wore a mismatched pair of sweatpants and a shirt and looked as if she'd rushed to dress in the first thing she could find.

So far, neither Logan nor Roy, the town's sheriff, who also happened to be Logan's uncle, had asked me to wait outside. I was sure that would change if I tried to move from my current location.

All the overhead lights in the shop had been turned on, but the additional illumination didn't ease the ominous undertones filling the air. The place might seem scary, but I was thankful to be waiting somewhere warm. Not having a ghost to help didn't stop me from being curious about the recent murder. I hoped to pick up some details about the man's death that I wouldn't be able to overhear if I'd been waiting outside.

I couldn't hear what was being said, but with every question Logan asked, Nadine rubbed her arms and cast a nervous glance toward the area where we'd found the body. Thankfully, the corpse had been removed, but the pool of blood on the hardwood floor still remained. Nadine would have to hire someone to refinish the floor because no amount of cleanup would make the stain disappear. Too bad the memory of what happened would be much harder to erase. I couldn't get the images of the stranger out of my mind and kept hearing the squeaky sound the wheels made when he was rolled out on a gurney.

"Are you all right?" I turned at the sound of Jade's voice. The tension thrumming through my system eased when I saw her and Shawna heading toward me. Though I would've been grateful for their support, I was glad the rest of my family hadn't arrived.

Elliott had been posted outside to keep onlookers away from the crime scene. My friends and I had known him since high school. I didn't know what they'd said to get him to allow them inside, but I was glad he had. Though, if he received a scolding from Roy, he might regret his decision later.

My friends' arrival didn't go unnoticed by Logan. He frowned and shot an accusatory glare in my direction as if I'd purposely invited them to join me. I'd thought about sending a text but decided to wait until I got home to make a call. Mainly to prevent the reaction I was currently receiving from the detective. I might have taken the time to correct his assumption if he hadn't been busy handing out orders and securing the crime scene.

"I'm fine, thanks," I said.

"Are you sure?" Shawna stepped around Jade and pulled me into a tight hug. "Grams called to tell us you and Logan found a body."

I smiled at my grandmother and mumbled, "Of course she did." The woman could sometimes be frustrating, but she always looked out for my friends and me.

Shawna hunched toward me and lowered her voice. "So, who died?" She craned her neck, trying to get a better look at the back of the room. Since the body was already gone, and the area where the man had died was blocked from view by a display case, she couldn't see much.

I glanced toward Logan to make sure his attention was elsewhere. He had stepped a few feet away from Nadine and Grams to converse with Roy. "Do you remember the man arguing with Nadine about the dagger when we were shopping earlier?"

"The one who was kind of rude and left in a huff?" Jade asked.

"Yeah," I said. "It was him."

"Do you think he came back to get the dagger?" Shawna asked.

"Possibly," I said. "It would explain the broken glass but not how he got stabbed in the back."

"Whoa," Jade said, wincing. "Was it the same dagger?"

"No, the hilt looked different," I said.

Jade glanced across the store, then asked, "Does Logan have any idea who he was?"

"Not that I'm aware of." The more I wondered about the man's identity, the more questions I had. Like why did he want the dagger so badly? Was he responsible for the break-in? Or was he passing by and interrupted the thief? Being in the wrong place at the wrong time could be a coincidence, which I found hard to believe.

"So, we don't even know if he's from around here," Jade said.

"Pretty sure he's not," Shawna said.

"Why would you say that?" Jade asked.

Shawna shrugged. "Nadine's pretty popular. I don't think there's anyone in town who hasn't gone to see her,"—she rolled her green eyes at me—"except maybe you."

I found it hard to believe I was the only local who wasn't interested in having their future foretold, but now was not the time to argue the point.

"Do you think finding a dead guy in the shop is going to impact Nadine's business in a bad way?" Shawna asked.

"Shawna," Jade groaned.

"What?" Shawna asked. "It's a legitimate question."

I shook my head. "I understand, but this probably isn't the best place to ask it." I didn't think Nadine needed to be concerned. My Uncle Max's business picked up after a body was found floating in the water near his boat in Cumberpatch's harbor.

Nadine might be strong and resilient, but I still worried about her. It was bad enough that someone she possibly knew had broken into her shop. Finding out a person she'd recently met had been murdered in a place that was special to her had to be traumatizing.

"Wait." Jade scrunched her brows as if a new thought had occurred to her. "Does Logan think Nadine is involved?"

"I don't know." My logical side knew Logan had to consider Nadine a suspect as part of his job. My emotional and protective side was annoyed with him for even considering the possibility that she could have killed anyone.

Jade interpreted my response as an affirmative and scowled. "Well, we'll have to prove him wrong."

I knew where this was going and cringed.

"Did you happen to find anything near the body that might have belonged to the dead guy?" Shawna asked.

"You mean like something I could use to summon one of my special visitors?" I asked.

"Yeah, like that," Shawna said, her voice ringing with enthusiasm. Even Jade was bobbing her head, hopeful at the prospect of helping me with a new ghost.

"No, and I didn't search the floor or go through his pockets looking for anything either." Touching a dead person was too morbid to think about. And I wouldn't have done it even if Logan had approved.

Shawna received a text, which I assumed, by her grin, was from Nate. He was always impressing her by sending cute emojis.

"Was that from Nate?" Jade asked, trying to sneak a peek over Shawna's shoulder.

"Nope," Shawna said, blocking Jade's view. As soon as she tucked her phone back in her jacket pocket, she made eye contact with Grams, then subtly shook her head.

I had a feeling the two of them were up to something, but I had no idea what it could be. Before I could voice my suspicions, Shawna inched toward a nearby brown mahogany table covered with a variety of glassware. A few seconds later, a porcelain lamp, which happened to be sitting near the edge, toppled to the floor.

A loud thud and the sound of shattering glass filled the

room and drew everyone's attention.

"Oh my gosh, I'm so sorry," Shawna said, pushing away from the table and spinning around. Her apologetic motions were over-dramatized, making me wonder if the lamp's demise had been an accident. "If somebody can get me a broom, I'd be happy to clean up the mess."

Identical glares erupted on Roy's and Logan's faces. They definitely weren't happy that Shawna had damaged their crime scene. Roy crossed his arms and glared at all of us, making me squirm. It reminded me of our high school days when guilt by association was the sheriff's mode of dealing with us whenever we got into trouble.

Logan straightened his shoulders and pursed his lips as he stalked toward my friends and me. I'd expected him to reprimand Shawna; instead, he placed his hand on my arm and said, "Can I talk to you for a minute." After I nodded, he urged me toward a spot away from the front door. "I'm afraid I won't be able to finish our date. It looks like I'm going to be here for a while."

"I understand," I said. I could eat dessert anytime, but after seeing a dead body, I'd lost my appetite. Logan and I were now focused on the murder, each of us with a different reason. I was no longer in the mood to spend the remainder of the evening curled up on my couch watching a movie, and it sounded like he wasn't either.

"I'd appreciate it if you let Elliott give you and your friends a ride home." Logan may have softened his tone, but it was laced with an underlying command. Because of Shawna's stunt, we were officially being removed from the premises.

I credited Logan's perception skills with his ability to understand people and say the right thing to get them to do what he wanted. He knew I was independent when it came to taking care of myself, so I had to give him points for how he'd turned his order into a request. Overseeing a murder investigation was probably easier than dealing with my grandmother since I was certain Grams wouldn't leave until the police were finished with Nadine.

Exhaustion from a long day combined with the possibility of a murderer lurking nearby was enough incentive to comply. "Okay."

"Barnes," Logan said, raising his arm and motioning with his fingers. "Can you make sure these ladies get home safely?"

CHAPTER FOUR

After Elliott dropped me off at my apartment, getting a good night's sleep had been difficult. It was hard to keep images of the man's body from popping into my mind. So far, his interest in obtaining the dagger was the only thing I knew about him.

Though I'd set the alarm to ensure I got up on time, I rarely had to wait for the buzzer to sound. My cat Barley woke up right before the first rays of sunlight peeked around the edges of the blinds covering my bedroom window. He then started pawing my head and any other patch of skin not hidden beneath my comforter.

"Morning," I said, gathering him on my chest and smoothing his long, gray and black-striped hair. After a few sharp-nailed flexes and a nose butt to my chin, Barley started purring. He was a Kurilian Bobtail and reminded me of a wild cat, minus a tail, and always having a bad hair day. I'd adopted the lovable furball when my first ghostly encounter with his previous owner had left him homeless.

The day beckoned, so I forced myself out of bed and proceeded through my usual routine, which included feeding Barley before he started making kitty noises that reached the level of shrilling.

Since I wasn't much of a cook and preferred grabbing something from Mattie's place across the street, getting ready didn't take long.

Even if the weather was bad, the only hardship I faced when heading to work was carrying my cat as I ascended the stairs to the door leading into the back of my family's shop.

As soon as I unclipped Barley's leash from his collar and set him on the ground, he took off down the hallway that led to the store in the front of the building. After stopping by my office to deposit my purse and leave my jacket on the hook behind the door, I followed him.

Though my parents sometimes liked to hang out in the store, I hadn't expected them to be here this early. They'd retired over a year ago, leaving me in charge of managing the shop as well as my grandmother. They spent most of their time traveling or doing personal things. Jade hadn't arrived yet, but Grams was standing behind the counter, prepping the cash register. "Good morning, sweetie," she said, glancing over her shoulder.

Apparently, my grandmother hadn't had any luck getting any sleep either. Her face had a lighter pallor, and the skin below her eyes was shadowed. At least her hair was neatly combed, and the ankle-length black skirt with a floral print she was wearing complimented her burnt-orange sweater.

"Hey," I said. "How's Nadine doing?" Knowing Grams, she'd already called her friend this morning to check in on her.

"Better than last night." She pushed the drawer shut and turned to face me. "What happened is horrible, and she needs our help." Grams furrowed her brows. "Especially if Roy and Logan think she had anything to do with that man's death." Roy was also one of her longtime friends, which made things even harder for her.

"What did they say?" I asked.

"It's not what they said, but how they acted when they

questioned her."

"Grams." I gave her arm a gentle squeeze. "I'm not happy about the situation either, but I think they're both just doing their jobs." Now that I wasn't standing in the middle of a crime scene and wasn't allowing my emotions to interfere, I could see things more objectively. It didn't mean I wouldn't voice my opinion should either man decide Nadine was capable of murder.

"Maybe," she harrumphed.

I quirked a brow. "So, did you overhear anything useful?" My grandmother was sharp and rarely missed a thing. Since she'd stayed behind with Nadine, I was hoping she'd learned the man's name or picked up something else that might be useful.

Even though the dead guy's ghost wasn't around for me to help, I still wanted to do whatever I could to prove Nadine's innocence without getting in Logan's way.

Helping a spirit find their killer eventually meant access to additional insight and information. I was determined to help Nadine any way I could, but without the dead man's help, or rather his ghost's, I wasn't sure how to proceed.

"No." Grams groaned. "The boys were pretty tight-lipped after you girls left. Logan asked a few more questions, then sent us on our way too."

If Logan planned to discuss anything important with Roy about his case, he'd been smart enough to make sure none of us were around to hear it.

I noticed that the "Open" side of the sign hanging on the front door was still facing inward, and asked, "Have you unlocked the door yet?"

Grams shook her head. "No. Would you mind?"

"Not at all."

On my return trip along the aisle, I noticed Barley batting something gold along the hardwood floor, its shiny surface glinting when it slid across a patch of sunlight. My cat was notorious for knocking the plastic bottles containing my mother's herbal remedies off the lower shelf. Other than napping on the shelf near the ceiling on the wall behind the counter holding the register, he didn't bother anything else in the store.

I wondered if he'd found something a customer had dropped. "What have you got there?" I crouched beside him and snatched an oval-shaped brooch containing an ivory-carved cameo of a Victorian woman off the floor before Barley could swat it again.

My grandmother and mother owned some antique jewelry, but I'd never seen this particular piece before and didn't think it belonged to either of them.

Unhappy that I'd ended his fun, Barley swatted my leg, then sauntered toward the next aisle. I didn't get a chance to ponder the owner's identity further. Seconds after my fingertips made contact with the metal's cool surface, a tingle zipped across my skin, sending an electrical shock all the way to my elbow. Thankfully, the sensation wasn't painful; otherwise, I would've tossed the brooch in the air.

I shook my head and groaned. Another ghost was coming, and there was absolutely nothing I could do to stop it. New ghosts struggled with their transition and didn't always appear immediately. I had no clue who was going to show up or how long I'd have to wait.

Then I remembered Shawna's so-called accident the night before and knew my instincts had been right. She'd purposely knocked the glass lamp on the floor and caused a distraction for my grandmother.

I suppose things could've been worse, and I should be grateful that Grams hadn't arrived in time to yank the dagger out of the dead guy's body. Not that Logan or Roy would've let her get away with it. I didn't think even her long-time friendship with the sheriff would keep either one of the men from throwing her in jail.

Extremely unhappy that I'd been outmaneuvered by a family member again, I spun around and glared at my grandmother. "Grams," I snarled. "I can't believe you used my cat to get me to summon a spirit."

"We need your special gift if we want to help Nadine," Grams huffed and crossed her arms. "I knew you'd refused to touch it if I tried to hand it to you."

"And you'd be right," I snapped, then placed the brooch on the counter in front of her. "How do you know this belonged to the dead guy?" It seemed odd that the deceased would own a piece of women's jewelry. I couldn't help worrying about the identity of my upcoming visitor or that they'd have nothing to do with the recent death.

"I didn't." Grams shrugged. "It was lying on the floor close to the spot where the body had been, so I figured there was a good chance the man touched it before he died."

I was still in the learning phase when it came to ghostly encounters. A person's possession was a good transmitter for my unique ability, but I had no idea if simply touching something before a person died would work.

My grandmother meant well, but calling a spirit wasn't the same as purchasing an article of clothing. You couldn't return a ghost if you didn't like it.

I closed my eyes and rubbed my forehead, searching for calm. A familiar drop in temperature, a precursor to an appearance, filled the air.

"Can you feel that?" Grams asked, rubbing the sleeves covering her arms and slowly lifting the ends of her lips to form a smug smile.

"Yeah," I said, opening my eyes. Memories of the chilling experience I'd had the last time my hand had passed through a spirit popped into my mind, and I took a step back in case the ghost appeared right next to me.

The area in the aisle leading to the front door shimmered a translucent blue and eventually transformed into a ghost. A ghost that looked nothing like the guy from Nadine's shop. In fact, it was an elderly woman who might have been close to my grandmother's age. She was tall with a slim figure and wore a light tan, ankle-length dress covered with small pastel flowers in shades of blue, pink, and white.

I still hadn't figured out why a spirit's clothes didn't have the same ethereal appearance as their bodies.

Hers wasn't the usual brilliant blue I associated with new spirits, but it hadn't lost much of its luster either. If she'd been dead for a long time, her color would've faded to a dull shade.

Her hair was pulled into a tight bun at her nape, her appearance reminding me of Ada Zimmerman, my sixth-grade teacher. That woman was unpleasant, and I couldn't think of anyone, my parents included, who viewed her as a decent role model. Her raspy voice and stern tone were enough to make children tremble. I might not be a child anymore, but thinking about the uppity woman always made me shudder, and I hoped my new ghost wasn't anything like her.

"Did it work?" Grams asked expectantly.

"No, I'd say we've got a bit of a situation." It was a huge problem, but I didn't share my opinion because I was afraid to frighten the bewildered spirit.

"Which is?" she asked.

"The brooch definitely didn't belong to the dead guy."

"Are you sure?" Grams asked. Her disappointed frown suggested that she thought it was my fault we'd gotten the wrong ghost.

I shot a menacing glare in her direction. Any admonishing comments I was about to share were cut off when the woman asked, "Excuse me, miss, but do you know where I am?"

"You're in the Mysterious Baubles, my family's shop," I said, hoping to alleviate the concern I'd heard in her voice. "I'm Rylee." I pointed at Grams. "And this is Abigail, my grandmother." My friends and I were the only ones who used the endearing nickname.

"But you can call me Abby," Grams said, even though I was the only one who could see the ghost.

"Um, it's nice to meet you," the woman said. "My

name is Cora."

I was also the only one who could hear whatever a spirit had to say, and for anyone who knew about my ability, I had to repeat everything I heard. Which, at times, could be fairly annoying.

"Her name is Cora," I told my grandmother.

Cora took a few steps closer, then, in an attempt to be polite, she lowered her voice and asked, "Does Abby have trouble hearing?"

"No," I said, stifling a snort and the temptation to tell Cora my grandmother could hear better than most people. She was just selective about what she chose to retain.

"Do you know how you got here?" I asked, hoping Cora knew she was dead because I dreaded having to tell her. Some new spirits were prone to hysterics after hearing the bad news. Not that I blamed them. Learning that your life was over couldn't be easy, and I spent a considerable amount of time wondering how I'd react if our roles were reversed.

If Cora knew she was deceased, would she know where she's been? Had she been locked away in some kind of spirit limbo? I tried not to think about the number of ghosts who might be trapped near the area where they died and weren't able to move on because no one could see or help them.

"Not really," Cora said absently, her gaze drawn to the counter behind me. "What are you doing with my brooch?" She flitted past me, leaving a chill in her wake. Her hand passed through the wooden frame when she tried to pick it up. "Well darn," she tsked. "It seems nothing's changed."

"What do you mean 'nothing's changed'?" I asked. I was pretty sure Cora was referring to her status as a ghost, but I wanted clarification in case I missed something.

"Apparently, I'm still dead," Cora said. "Does that mean you are too?"

Before I could answer, Grams drew my attention by

tapping her fingernails on the glass counter and asking, "Care to fill me in?" She seemed to have lost her patience at not being kept in the ghostly conversation loop.

Cora shot me another confused look since I hadn't answered her earlier question about my grandmother's hearing.

"No, I'm not dead, and neither is my grandmother," I said to Cora. "Unfortunately, I'm the only one who can see and hear you."

"Are you the one who brought me here?" Cora asked.

In times like this, I regretted having very little knowledge about ghostly entities and wished I'd hear back about my application for sleuther training. "Yes," I said. "I have a special ability, but I'm not entirely sure how the traveling part works." I added the last part to keep her from asking questions I couldn't answer.

I did know that if I failed to resolve her death, she'd be stuck haunting me for the rest of my life. An important fact I wasn't willing to share, at least not yet. Knowing Cora could disappear any minute motivated me to ask more pertinent questions. "Do you know where you live?"

"Of course, I know where I live," Cora snapped.

"I mean, can you tell me the address?"

"Oh, yes, it's—"

The click of heels on the hardwood floor echoing from the hallway meant Jade had arrived. Too bad the noise startled Cora, and she vanished. New ghosts also had difficulty controlling their movements, so I had no idea when she'd reappear.

"What happened?" Jade asked. Either she'd heard my groan or glimpsed my disappointed expression.

"I received a visit from a new ghost." Pointing at the brooch and glaring at my grandmother was all the explanation Jade needed for guilt to flush her cheeks and cause her to ramble. "I know I should've called, but after we got home, Shawna swore me to secrecy before telling me her little mishap wasn't an accident."

If my friend had provided me with a warning, I would've been able to thwart my grandmother's meddling and wouldn't have been stuck with a ghost who had nothing to do with the murder in Nadine's shop.

Shawna, Jade, and I had been best friends for what seemed like forever, and I knew I could count on both of them no matter what happened. Making promises and guarding secrets were oaths we took seriously. Even so, it didn't stop me from being annoyed or narrowing my gaze at Jade.

"I'm really sorry," Jade said. "I'll do whatever I can to help."

"You can count me in as well," Grams said, her remorse-laden voice making it hard to cast more blame or stay mad at her. Instead, I told Jade about Cora's arrival and relayed everything she'd said.

When the bell hanging above the front door tinkled, I'd expected to turn and find a customer, not Shawna strolling into the shop. "Hey, everyone," she said. After glancing at each of our faces, she asked, "What'd I miss?"

Her blue-streaked, light-brown curls were pulled back into a ponytail. She was dressed in her work uniform, which consisted of a black skirt and cobalt-blue T-shirt. Below her shoulder, on the left side of her shirt, was the logo for the Cumberpatch Cove Cantina; a pirate ship with the restaurant's name printed across the center of it.

"You mean besides my grandmother tricking me into summoning another ghost?" I asked.

"Way to go, Grams," Shawna said. She glanced around the store as if she expected a spirit to magically appear. "Is it the dead guy from Nadine's place? Was he able to tell you what happened to him?"

Jade slapped her hands on her hips. "No. Your distraction maneuver backfired."

"What?" Shawna asked, her smile fading.

"I'm afraid the brooch I grabbed belonged to someone else," Grams said. It was the closest she'd come to apologizing since luring me into her debacle. "Her name is Cora, and we have no idea how she died."

Shawna widened her eyes. "Did you get a last name or find out where she lives?" She'd turned surfing the Internet into an art form and no doubt planned to gather whatever information she could about Cora. "How about her connection to Nadine's place?"

"I didn't get to ask her any of those questions," I said. "She poofed out before I had a chance."

Shawna sighed. "Well, that's too bad."

"Tell me about it," I said. Our newest ghostly adventure was off to a terrible start. A first name and a cameo brooch weren't much to go on. Without knowing Cora's last name, we couldn't research where she lived, how she died, or if anyone had ever found her body. The design of her clothes suggested she lived in the current century, so I didn't think I was dealing with someone who'd been cursed. At least I hoped not. Though with each new tidbit I discovered about the area's witching community, I assumed anything was possible.

Besides feeling the heavy weight of solving the mystery behind Cora's death, we still needed to help Nadine. Compiling everything my friends and I had learned so far, which wasn't much, wasn't getting us any closer to finding any killers.

CHAPTER FIVE

Until Cora reappeared, I couldn't do anything to help her. In the meantime, my friends and I decided to meet at my place after work to see what we could do about Nadine's situation.

I'd never tried to solve two murders simultaneously, and the lack of information raised my level of stress. On the positive side, I only had to deal with one ghost. Though with Nadine being one of my grandmother's closest friends, I was sure she'd make up for the lack of an additional spirit.

I wasn't much of a cook, so when we got together, we usually ordered takeout. Not long after the pizza was delivered, Grams and Nadine arrived. None of us were heavy drinkers, but after everything that had happened, we welcomed the wine coolers my grandmother brought with her.

My parents had other plans but asked me to make sure I told Nadine they were thinking about her and to let them know if she needed anything. I hadn't told either of them about my visit from Cora. My father was worse than my grandmother when it came to a spirit's arrival. He'd have plenty of questions, so I didn't want to tell him until I talked with Cora and could answer them.

I wasn't a criminal, nor did I want to be one, but sometimes solving ghost-related crimes required utilizing creative techniques that weren't necessarily considered lawful. Keeping my parents out of the loop provided them with deniability. It also gave me two less people to worry about should something go wrong, like being caught and possibly ending up in jail.

I'd given up trying to exclude Grams. No matter how hard I tried, she somehow managed to find out what my friends and I were up to. My grandmother was convinced she received psychic premonitions in her dreams. None of her forecasts had ever amounted to anything, so up until recently, I'd scoffed at her predictions.

The living room and kitchen shared a large open space. Though my table seated four, my friends and I rarely used it for meals.

After opening the pizza boxes and placing napkins and plastic utensils on the coffee table, Jade slipped off her shoes and settled into the cushioned chair. Shawna plopped down in her usual spot on the right end of the couch. My sofa could easily seat three, so I grabbed a kitchen chair and let Grams and Nadine have the other two spots.

I'd already fed Barley, but the prospect of more food had him jumping up on the couch and squeezing in between Nadine and Shawna. My cat possessed stellar stealth abilities. He wasn't allowed to have table scraps. I had to keep a watchful eye on him and Shawna, who occasionally gave into his intense scrutiny and tried to sneak him a crumb or two.

"How are you doing?" I asked Nadine as I picked up a plate and snagged a slice.

She unscrewed the cap of her peach-flavored cooler and sighed. "All right, I guess. Yesterday wasn't exactly the day I envisioned."

"How long will it take before they let you open again?"

Jade asked.

I felt bad for Nadine. Now that her new place was a crime scene, she wouldn't be able to finish her sale or move forward with renovations.

"Roy couldn't give me an exact date but said he'd push things along as much as he could," Nadine said. "He thought it might be a couple more days."

"Let's hope so," Grams said.

She and the sheriff might be good friends, but I'd always suspected that Roy wished the two of them were closer. If my grandmother got involved, I had no doubt he'd help move things along even faster to keep her from pestering him. I didn't miss the mischievous glint in her eyes confirming that I was right.

"What about the damage to the front door?" I asked.

Nadine set her drink on the table. "It's already been boarded up, so I won't have to worry about anyone else breaking in."

"Could you tell if anything was stolen?" I asked.

"Not without doing an in-depth inventory, which I'll do after Logan gives me the okay to go back into the shop," she said.

"Did you already call Nathan and let him know what happened?" Grams asked.

Nadine nodded. "Yes. He didn't sound very happy, but he did agree to let Aaron stay longer."

"That's good," I said. I'd never met Nathan and had no idea if he genuinely wanted to help or if he wanted Aaron to stick around and keep an eye on things to ensure he received his portion of the profit.

After a few minutes of silence, where everyone busied themselves with eating, Nadine set her empty plate on the coffee table and said, "I understand you have a new visitor, but not the one *someone* was hoping for." She cast a sidelong glance at Grams.

Grams must have shared details with Nadine about Cora's arrival. It didn't sound like she'd known anything about Grams and Shawna's conspiracy or that she'd approved of what they'd done any more than I had.

"I did," I said. "I'm hoping she shows up soon so I can ask her more questions." Thinking about Cora reminded me about her brooch. "We need to give her brooch back to Logan." Even if the killer had touched the piece of jewelry, I doubted the police would get any fingerprints from it, not after Grams and I had handled it. Even so, I put the brooch in a plastic bag.

"Why?" Grams asked. "We know it didn't belong to his victim."

"Because it's still part of his crime scene." Logan was going to be angry, and I wasn't looking forward to the visit. I thought about making my grandmother go with me so she could personally explain her actions to him. Then I began imagining all the things that could go wrong if she was involved and decided to make the trip to the station alone.

Grams slumped her shoulders and groaned. "I suppose you're right." She was probably trying to devise a decent excuse to give Roy when he found out. I pressed my lips together to keep from grinning. That was one conversation I wouldn't mind overhearing.

"It's a shame you didn't get a chance to give the dead guy a reading," Shawna said. "Maybe then he wouldn't have ended up on your floor with a dagger sticking out of his back."

"Shawna," Jade growled through gritted teeth. My friend didn't come with a filter and usually said whatever was on her mind. Since they shared an apartment, Jade was around Shawna a lot more than me and was also the one who scolded her the most. I was afraid the creases on her forehead would be permanently etched by the time Jade reached her fifties.

Shawna ignored her and leaned forward to grab another slice of pizza. I envied her high metabolism and the amount of food she could consume without gaining weight. If I didn't get a lot of exercise working in the shop, my passion for sweets would be a problem. As it was, the lack of a slimming height added a few more pounds than I'd like to my hips.

"It's okay." Nadine dismissed Shawna's comment with a chuckle. In her line of work, she probably heard a lot worse. "Even if I had given the man a reading, I'm afraid it doesn't work like that." She took a long swallow of her drink. "I get a general sense of things that could happen. I don't always receive a mental image, and if I do, it doesn't mean what I see will definitely happen. The choices a person makes with the information I provide can still alter their path."

"That's too bad," Shawna said. "It would've been nice if you could use your crystal ball and see his killer."

Nadine gave a half-hearted laugh. "I'd probably be a rich woman if I had that kind of talent."

"It also would've been nice if we had a ghost that could actually help us," Jade said sarcastically as she traded her empty plate for her wine cooler.

Jade was still annoyed about her role in the current mess Shawna and Grams had created. A mess she could've prevented if she hadn't sworn not to say anything to me. Since refereeing came with our friendship, I was good at stopping arguments before they got started.

Grams was quicker to change the subject. "Speaking of ghosts, have you seen any sign of Cora yet?"

"No," I said. I'd had other spirits tell me I was like a lighthouse beacon, that they could always find me, so I knew Cora would eventually make an appearance. It was when and where that concerned me. A ghost showing up at an inopportune moment had happened on more than one occasion.

So far, none of them had arrived in my bedroom or in my bathroom while I was taking a shower. Martin had been the only one I truly worried about. His devious side had prompted me to set ground rules.

"I know you need to find out what happened to Cora, but you're still planning on helping us, right?" Grams asked.

Everyone in the room knew about the afterlife time constraint. I wasn't sure exactly when it had happened, but sometime during one of our adventures, the group collectively started looking to me for leadership.

"Of course, I'm going to help," I said. "But Logan's not going to be happy after I return the brooch, so we need to be careful about how we get involved in his case."

Shawna snorted. "When has being under his scrutiny ever stopped us?"

Thinking back, I knew it hadn't.

"When you were being questioned by Logan, did he happen to mention if they'd identified the victim?" Shawna asked. I'd forgotten that she hadn't been around when I'd asked Grams the same question earlier that morning.

Roy and Logan would eventually have to share the information with the public, but not until after they'd contacted the man's relatives. I figured we'd have to wait until something appeared in the next issue of the *Swashbuckler Gazette*. Troy Duncan, the newspaper's only reporter, had pestered my friends and me a few times in the past, so I knew he was tenacious about getting details for his articles.

"No, he asked us to leave not long after you left," Grams said.

Knowing my grandmother and her penchant for scheming, she was probably hoping she could snag a few more items to ensure I summoned the dead guy's ghost.

Grams held her bottle several inches from her mouth. "And you can bet if he hadn't sent Elliott along with you, I could've gotten something out of him."

Of that, I had no doubts. Elliott knew better than to share what he'd learned with anyone, specifically my friends and me. When plied with the right incentive, he'd been known to inadvertently drop a useful clue. If I wanted to use him as a source again, I'd need to find a way to run into him outside the station.

Thinking about Grams gathering whatever baubles she could find reminded me of Cora and her brooch. Maybe tracking down how the piece of jewelry ended up in the shop might lead us to where it had come from. It also wouldn't hurt to find out whatever I could about the dagger. "Did Hildie keep a log or database that listed where she purchased the items she sold?" I asked Nadine, hoping she had a computer system, something we could easily access.

"From what I could tell, she stored everything on her computer," Nadine said. "Since I plan to keep anything, I only accessed the inventory data, not where each item originated. I did find a ledger underneath a stack of files in her desk but didn't bother verifying the information since I assumed she'd already entered it in the computer."

I hadn't known Hildie well, but from our interactions, I'd gleaned that she was smart, organized, and quite the salesperson. There had to be a reason she kept a separate log, and I'd bet they pushed the boundaries of anything legal. "Did Logan or Roy ask you about the information or confiscate the ledger?" I asked.

"No, I didn't tell them about the ledger because they were more interested in what had been taken from the store and what I knew about the victim," Nadine said.

"Is the ledger still in your office?" I asked.

"Yes, but they won't let me into the building until they release the crime scene." Nadine patted the sofa's armrest. "And, like I said, the guys couldn't give me a definite date."

I crumpled my napkin as I got up to grab the empty paper plates stacked on the coffee table and dispose of them in the trashcan underneath the kitchen sink. I returned to my seat and nearly walked through Cora's translucent form. "Hey, Cora," I said after recovering from my shock and also to alert the others. I tipped my head in her direction so everyone would know where she was standing.

Her hair was still pulled back in a bun, and she was wearing an ankle-length dress similar to the one she'd had on before, only this one was white and covered with bright orange poppies.

Cora glanced around the room and wrinkled her nose. "Showing up in places I've never been is disconcerting. I assume it's because of that special ability you mentioned before."

"Sorry about that, but yes," I said.

"It's all right. I was tired of being stuck in my house anyway." Cora smiled. "So, where am I now?"

"You're in my apartment above my family's shop," I said.

She gazed around the room appreciatively, then wiggled her finger at the group. "I recognize Abby, but who are these other people?"

"These are my friends; Jade, Shawna, and Nadine." I pointed at each of them as I provided their names.

My friends reciprocated by saying "Hey" or "Hello."

In case Cora's stay was cut short, I decided to get an answer to the most important question first. "The last time we spoke, I didn't get your surname."

Cora hesitated, then said, "Why? Is it important?"

"I didn't get a chance to tell you that my main goal is helping you find the person who ended your life." I was afraid she'd worry, so I left out the part about it being time sensitive.

"Knowing your full name will help with any research we do," I said. Her tight-lipped expression eased, but only a little. Even if she was dead, I could understand her not wanting to believe a stranger. To be successful, I needed her to trust me. "If it helps, my boyfriend is also a detective with the local police force." Though technically, Logan wouldn't be assisting us.

Luckily, Cora drew the conclusion I'd hoped for

because she relaxed her rigid stance and said, "My last name is Emerson."

"Emerson," I repeated for the group, then asked, "Cora, can you remember what happened the night you...died?"

"I was supposed to go out to dinner with some of my friends, but I wasn't feeling well and decided to stay home and go to bed early." Cora rubbed her arms. I didn't think she was actually experiencing chills but rather an emotional response to her recollections. "I heard noises like someone moving around downstairs, so I went down to investigate."

I relayed what Cora said.

"Why didn't you call the police and stay in your bedroom where it was safe?" Shawna asked.

Cora scrunched her face, no doubt offended by my friend's question. "I would have, except I'd left my phone in the kitchen."

Cora might be unable to fully control her actions and could poof out at any time. I had more questions and decided to keep her on track rather than explain that Shawna wasn't trying to be condescending or hurtful. She just had a direct way of handling things. "What happened when you went downstairs to find your phone and investigate?"

Repeating conversations wasn't fun. I was glad my friends had gotten good at following along if I supplied them with enough information.

"It was dark, so I turned on a light, thinking it might scare away whoever was down there," Cora said.

Obviously, since she was now a ghost, her efforts had failed. I hated making anyone relive gruesome details, but the more information I had, the more helpful I could be. "Would you mind telling us what happened after you turned on the light?"

Cora shook her head as if trying to dislodge a painful memory. "I'm not sure. I remember glimpsing something moving in my periphery, then nothing until I woke up like this." She swept her hands along the front of her body.

I shared what she'd said. Judging by their disappointed expressions, they weren't any happier than I was to learn that Cora hadn't seen her killer.

"Cora, I'm so sorry this happened to you," Nadine said, her voice consoling. "Everyone here, myself included, will do whatever we can to help you find whoever was responsible for your death."

"Absolutely," Shawna said.

Cora received smiles and head nods from the others.

If ghosts could cry, I was sure I'd see clear blue tears trickling down her face. "I don't know how to thank you." Cora sniffled, then, without saying another word, she disappeared.

What she'd told me wasn't much, but it was a start. Hopefully, the next time Cora showed up, I could find out where she lived so I could follow up and make sure the police had found her body.

Now that we had Cora's full name, Shawna might be able to find some details about her past, and I might get some information from Logan. The latter depended on how well things went when I turned over the brooch.

I must've been staring at the spot where Cora was standing longer than I'd thought because after clearing her throat, Jade raised a brow expecting me to fill them in with the latest tidbit she'd given me. "Sorry, guys. I'm afraid Cora poofed out again, so that's all we're going to get for now."

CHAPTER SIX

After Cora disappeared the night before, Shawna and Jade hung around after Grams and Nadine left so we could discuss what to do with the information we'd learned so far. Unfortunately, we had no good ideas and eventually decided to call it a night.

With Logan in the middle of a murder investigation, I didn't know if he'd be at the station or out searching for clues. It would've been easy to devise an excuse not to hand in the brooch and avoid the confrontation and lecture I knew was coming.

If it turned out the brooch was important, the longer I held onto it, the more trouble it would cause Grams. My mother believed, as I did, that people should be held accountable for their actions. She'd probably agree wholeheartedly that a night in jail would be good for Grams. I loved my grandmother, and no matter how much trouble she caused, I wasn't willing to let her be locked up.

After texting Logan and arranging a time to meet in the afternoon, I spent the morning working at the shop. Because of the high tourist traffic our town received, staying busy hadn't been difficult.

Other than Anthony, the officer sitting at the desk

behind the counter, the reception area in the police station was empty. He'd also grown up in Cumberpatch, was a few years younger than me, and had only been working at the station for a little over a year.

He looked up from what he was doing and smiled. "Hey, Rylee. How's it going?" Anthony's sandy blond hair was cropped above his ears. He had a tall build, and because he worked out regularly, a fact he'd shared with me on numerous occasions, his muscles stretched the fabric of his uniform.

"Fine, I think," I said.

"I take it you're here to see Logan."

After a few visits to the station, it didn't take long for his coworkers to figure out we were dating. I hitched the strap of my purse higher up on my shoulder. "Yeah, he's expecting me."

"Why don't you take a seat," he said, reaching for the phone on his desk. "And I'll let him know you're here."

"Thanks." I barely had a chance for my backside to warm the cold bench before Logan strolled into the room with a welcoming grin.

"Hey, come on back," he said, motioning me to follow him. I understood his need to appear professional around his underlings and wasn't disappointed that I didn't receive a customary hug or kiss from him. Outside of the office, he never failed to show affection. Not that I was insecure or doubted his commitment to our relationship.

I followed Logan to the back of the building, where his office was located. When he reached the open doorway, he stepped aside and placed his hand on the small of my back, urging me to go ahead of him. Once inside, he closed the door and ran his hands along my arms. "Are you doing okay?"

I didn't have to ask to know he was referring to my emotional well-being after seeing the gruesome state of the man's body two nights ago. I didn't think I'd ever reach a point where seeing death firsthand wouldn't bother me, but at least it wasn't as unsettling as it used to be. "I'm all right."

His dark gaze held mine for a few moments longer, then, as if satisfied with what he saw, he perched on the end of his desk.

I studied the exhaustion tinging his features and wondered if he'd been sleeping any better than I had. "How about you?" I asked as I settled into one of the two chairs meant for visitors.

"Tough case," he said. The change in his expression was subtle, but I could already tell that he'd reverted back to his detective mode.

"Any leads?" I asked out of curious habit.

"You know I enjoy seeing you, but I can't share any details."

"I know," I said, trying to keep the frustration out of my voice. "I'm actually here to give you something." I reached into my jacket pocket and wrapped my hand around the plastic bag containing the brooch. "But before I do, I need you to promise that you won't put Grams in jail for trying to help."

Logan was well aware of my grandmother's eccentric antics, so I wasn't surprised when he rolled his eyes. "I'm assuming it has to do with my case."

I nodded.

"Unless she's killed someone, I suppose I can overlook whatever she did." He held up a hand. "Provided she doesn't do anything else to interfere."

Relieved that my grandmother had escaped becoming a jailbird, I released a nervous chuckle. "No bodies and I promise I'll do everything I can to keep an eye on her." Other than locking Grams in a room until the culprit was found, it was the best I could offer.

His gaze shifted to my pocket, and he wiggled his fingers. "Okay, let's have it."

I pulled out the bag and handed it to him.

He held it up to examine the contents, then quirked a

brow. "What's this?"

I could feel the heat rising on my cheeks and forced myself to inhale a deep breath before answering. "It's evidence from your crime scene."

Logan rubbed his eyes and groaned. "I take it Shawna's incident with the lamp wasn't an accident, was it?"

It was bad enough having to admit what my grandmother had done, but I was loyal to my friends. I refused to get one of them in trouble, so I responded with a shrug.

After a long moment of silence in which I was certain he was contemplating whether or not to give Shawna a verbal warning, he asked, "Was there anything else?"

"Yeah." I twisted my hands in my lap, then said, "I may have accidentally summoned a ghost when I touched the brooch."

"May have?" Logan asked.

"Okay…did," I said, not wanting to admit that I'd been outmaneuvered by my grandmother.

"Is he here now?" With a look of expectation, Logan straightened and glanced around the room the same way Shawna always did, as if the spirit in question would automatically appear for him.

"No," I said, grimacing. "He is a she and *not* your murder victim."

"What?" Logan frowned. "How is that possible?" It didn't take him long to reach the same conclusion I had. "Are you telling me that you ended up with the ghost from another murder?"

"I'm afraid so," I said.

"Did she tell you her name?"

"Cora Emerson." I shifted uncomfortably in my seat. It would've been nice to have Cora hovering nearby to answer Logan's questions. Once again, I wished I'd hear back on my application. If I got accepted into the spirit sleuther program, one of the first things I planned to ask was whether or not there was a way to summon a ghost instead of waiting for them to randomly appear.

"I don't know where she lives or how long she's been dead," I said. "Though, judging by her clothes and the way she talked, I don't think it was that long ago. All I know for sure is that she's an older woman and has no idea how she died. And I don't know how she...I mean her brooch ended up in Nadine's shop."

"Wait a minute," Logan said. "Did you say her last name was Emerson?" He pushed off the desk and walked around to his chair. After setting the plastic bag aside, he faced his computer screen and tapped a few keys.

"Yes, why?"

"Because the man we found in Nadine's shop is Liam Emerson. And I don't believe in coincidences."

I wasn't a big believer in coincidences either. I eased to the edge of my seat, hoping that my grandmother's good intentions had actually succeeded.

Logan stared at the screen and scrolled with his mouse, then frowned. "According to Liam's file, his closest relative is his grandmother, Cora." He looked back at me. "It looks like your ghost and my murder victim are related."

I wasn't happy to hear that two members of the same family had lost their lives to unnatural deaths, but it was nice to finally gain a promising clue. Unfortunately, it also created more unanswered questions. Like how did the brooch end up on the floor in Nadine's new shop? What was Liam doing there? Was he the one who'd broken in so he could search for the dagger? Were his and Cora's deaths related? Who was responsible for taking their lives? And, more importantly, were we looking for more than one killer?

Logan had returned to speculatively staring at the screen. No doubt his thoughts were filled with questions similar to mine. Things would be much easier if Logan and I could work together, more specifically on his current case. Because of our personal relationship and the impact it might have on his job, it was a line I'd been adamant not to cross in the past. Though there'd been a few times that I'd brushed up against the boundary.

I was about to break my rule and ask Logan how he felt about joining forces when the phone on his desk rang and startled me into silence.

"Yes," Logan said.

I couldn't hear what the caller was saying, but his grim expression meant it must not have been good.

"I'll take care of it," Logan said, replacing the receiver. "I'm afraid we'll have to finish this later." He pushed out of his seat. "Old Clyde reported a problem and requested me to come out and handle it."

Clyde Anderson had worked as a caretaker at the By the Bay Cemetery for years.

"He probably thinks he saw Martin's ghost again, or there are some teenagers up to no good. Either way, I need to go," Logan said.

As far as I knew, Martin had moved on to his afterlife, so I was inclined to believe Logan would be dealing with pranksters. "No problem," I said, adjusting the strap of my purse as I got to my feet.

"We'll talk later." Logan pressed a kiss to my forehead before opening the door and escorting me out of the station.

A feeling of deja vu settled over me, and I hugged my chest. Though I didn't want to admit it, death seemed to play a role in our lives. The first time we'd met was because a dead body had been found in the graveyard. As I watched him drive away, I hoped that history wasn't repeating itself.

CHAPTER SEVEN

It was late afternoon by the time I'd returned to the shop after meeting with Logan and running a few errands. Part of me was almost glad our conversation had been interrupted because I wasn't sure if asking him to combine resources was the right thing to do.

Finding a guy who was okay with the peculiarities of my family, not to mention the fact that I could communicate with ghosts, was rare. Things between us were going well, and I didn't want to do something that might change it.

You'd think a small town like Cumberpatch wouldn't have enough crime to keep our local law enforcement busy, but we did. Maybe it was the underlying supernatural element or the continual flow of tourists that had never been seasonal or impacted by the weather. Or perhaps it was a combination of both. Whatever the motivation, I'd probably have another day or so before Logan and I could get together and talk again.

During the drive back to the shop, all I could think about was the familial ties between Cora and Liam. I hoped by helping Cora, my friends and I would inadvertently find a way to assist Liam as well. Their connection was a huge clue, and I couldn't wait to share it with my friends.

Knowing my persistent boyfriend, he'd probably check into Cora's death and search for a possible link with Liam's once he returned from his trip to see Clyde. It would've been nice if I'd gotten a little more information from Logan, like finding out where they lived.

Hopefully, the next time I spoke with Cora, she'd be able to provide the location. I would also need to tell her about Liam, something I truly dreaded. I didn't know anything about her relationship with her grandson. If they were close, finding out he'd died, and in such a horrific manner, would break Cora's heart.

After remaining in the car, contemplating and failing to come up with a subtle way to tell Cora what happened that wouldn't cause her to poof out permanently, I slipped inside the rear of the building.

With an hour left before closing, I stopped in the office long enough to drop off my purse, then headed for the shop.

"There you go," Jade said as she handed a bulky plastic bag that looked like it might contain books across the check-out counter to a middle-aged woman. Besides a nice selection of pirate lore, my father insisted we carry books covering different aspects of the supernatural. Surprisingly, those were the ones that sold the most. Before I'd been zapped with the ability to see spirits, I never had an interest in their contents. Now, I could honestly say I'd perused every one of them.

"Thanks," the woman said. "I can't wait to read these." She gave the bag a pat, then turned to leave. She wore a bright yellow T-shirt underneath her lightweight jacket. All I could see of the logo was a skull and crossbones and figured she must have visited one of the souvenir shops farther down the street.

The shop had a steady flow of customers most of the time, so part of our end-of-day routine included checking the shelves and restocking anything that had run low. I spotted Grams near the end of the main aisle realigning items.

"Hey," I said to both of them as I joined Jade behind the counter.

I received a "Hey, sweetie" from my grandmother and a "Hey back" from my friend.

Before any of us could say anything else, a ball of fur with legs sailed past my head and landed on the counter next to me. Grams chuckled, and Jade sucked in a breath and placed her hand on her chest. "Barley," she scolded. "You'd think I'd be used to him doing that by now."

"I know what you mean," I said, giggling. My nervous system hadn't gone unscathed by his stealthy arrival either. Not for lack of trying, but none of us could figure out how my cat reached the shelf near the ceiling.

Barley let out a welcoming meow and swiped at my arm, expecting to receive his usual head scratching. "Hey there, boy. How was your nap?" He responded with more purring, then head-butted my hand because I'd dared to stop petting him.

"So, using the number ten scale, how upset was Logan?" Jade asked since I'd told her and Grams where I was going before I left.

I glanced at Grams, who'd stopped what she was doing to give us her full attention. "He wasn't happy, but I won't have to bail *my grandmother* out of jail."

"Bail her out for what?" my mother's annoyed voice echoed from the other side of the room. I'd forgotten that my parents might be lurking about today. Some of the aisles were lined with shelves too high to see over, and I hadn't thought to check the rest of the store before answering Jade's question.

She appeared a few seconds later, glaring at Grams, then refocusing her intense brown gaze on me. Her hair was tucked into a messy bun on the top of her head, and the sleeves of her shirt were pushed up past her elbows.

According to my mother, springtime was meant for cleaning, which explained the dusting cloth clasped in her hand. She'd spend additional time working throughout the shop until the entire place glistened.

Of the two women who'd played important roles in my life, my mother, when angry, was the one I feared the most. And, since I strongly believed people should take responsibility for their actions, I clamped my lips together tightly and shot my grandmother a you're-on-your-own look.

Not to be outmaneuvered by me or anyone else, Grams crossed her arms and smiled sweetly, then said, "Maybe you should go first. I'm sure your parents would love to hear about your newest visitor."

Thanks to my grandmother's declaration, I was also going to have to explain why I waited so long to tell them about Cora. There were plenty of places my father could be hiding. I didn't want to share the details more than once and asked, "Is dad here?"

"He's in the storeroom," Grams said. "I'll go get him." She spun and headed for the hallway, amazing me once again at how fast a woman of her age could move, especially when she wanted to avoid a lecture.

Less than a minute later, I heard hurried footsteps coming from the hallway, and my father rushed into the room with Grams following closely behind him. He spotted me and grinned. "I understand you have some exciting news you'd like to share."

I could see by the sparkle in his eyes that he'd already gleaned it had something to do with a new spirit, and I couldn't bring myself to tell him that 'exciting' wasn't exactly how I'd describe what I needed to say.

I had to give my parents credit for being good listeners and not interrupting me to ask questions. Unfortunately for Grams, I couldn't explain how I'd summoned Cora without telling them about the brooch she'd taken from Nadine's shop. I did, however, leave out the part where my grandmother used my cat to trick me into picking the piece of jewelry up off the floor.

Shawna might have been complicit in helping Grams with her extraction, but she was my friend, and my parents adored her. After receiving a worried look from Jade, I decided to keep Shawna's name out of the story and out of trouble.

Once I was done, my mother snorted. "Honestly, Abigail, what made you think a piece of woman's jewelry would be linked to the unfortunate man they found at Nadine's new place?"

"Like I already told Rylee," Grams said defensively. "The brooch was on the floor in the same area the body had been, and it was the only thing I could grab without being seen."

"It was a crime scene," my mother said. "You shouldn't have been grabbing anything."

"I agree," I said, softening my tone. "But it's a good thing you did."

"What?" Grams said, widening her eyes.

"It turns out that Cora and the man who was murdered are related."

CHAPTER EIGHT

After Barley and I returned to our apartment, I set him on the floor and unclipped the leash from his collar. Without any additional information, moving forward with helping Cora presented numerous dilemmas. I could do an online search, but unless the websites provided a picture, I'd have no way of knowing whether or not I had the right person. "I have no idea what to do next," I said, bending over to scratch my cat's head. "Any suggestions?"

His kitty noises had nothing to do with answering my question. It was the sound he made when he was adamant about being fed. He strolled toward the cabinet where I kept the bag of his dry cat food, making sure to rub his side along the door on the way to his bowls.

I giggled as I reached inside and pulled out the bag. "You're obviously not going to be any help, are you?"

Barley sat on his haunches and replied with an impatient meow. A few seconds later, my name echoed through the room. When Cora appeared several inches away from me, I squeaked and flung my arms into the air. The bag flew from my hand, sailed through the middle of her chest, and opened as it thudded against the floor, providing an escape for the small fish-shaped tidbits stored inside.

I stared at the mess and groaned. Until now, I'd been doing reasonably well with ghosts popping in and out of my life and had gotten much better at controlling my reactions.

My cat pounced on the morsels. Barley might be picky about the brand of cat food he preferred, but he didn't seem to care where he ate his dinner.

"Barley, no," I said, moving him aside so I could scoop food off the floor and into his bowl, then returned the remainder to the bag.

"Sorry about that," Cora said. "I'm still having trouble controlling…things."

I didn't want her to stress unnecessarily, so I said, "Don't worry. It's not the first time I've spilled cat food on the floor." And it most likely wouldn't be the last. I stuck the bag back in the cabinet. "I'm actually glad you're here."

"You are?" Cora sounded surprised.

"Yes." I pulled two chairs away from the kitchen table and motioned for her to take a seat as I sat down on the other. "There's something I'd like to chat with you about."

Once settled, Cora asked, "Did you learn something new about my case?" She looked at me as if I was a professional she'd recently hired.

The only thing I was truly experienced with was running my family's shop. Being a part-time spirit sleuther came with challenges and rules that I was still trying to grasp.

"Sort of," I said. I didn't want her to disappear again, so I stared at my lap, trying to come up with the best way to relay the bad news about her grandson. Barley had finished eating and curled up in his favorite spot on the sofa.

"By the look on your face, I'm guessing whatever you have to say isn't good," Cora said, drawing my attention back to her face. "So just tell me."

I found myself hesitating. I had no reason to doubt the

information Logan found linking Liam and Cora, but I wanted to be absolutely sure before I told her he'd been murdered. "Okay," I sighed. "Do you know a man named Liam Emerson?"

"I have a grandson named Liam. He lives in Brindburrow. We both do, or in my case, did."

I vaguely recalled the town's name and was pretty sure it was somewhere along the coast or a little farther inland. Now that I had a location, I'd be able to do some research without asking Cora more questions and sparing her from reliving any more potentially painful experiences.

"Why?" Cora asked, her voice laced with concern. "Has something happened to him?"

I squelched the urge to reach for her hand and offer comfort. "Remember when we first met, and you asked about your brooch?"

"Yes, but then we got sidetracked with other things."

"We had your brooch because Grams found it on the floor of a crime scene." Seeing blood spilled on the floor would've been enough incentive to keep most people away. Unfortunately, my grandmother wasn't like most people and shared the same disregard for fear as Shawna.

Cora gasped. "Are you saying it was found by someone's body?" She widened her eyes. "Whose?"

Over the next few minutes, I explained how I'd first seen Liam in The Booty Bazaar and his interest in the dagger. I told her how Logan and I had found Liam but refrained from providing any descriptive details.

She listened intently without interrupting, though the longer I talked, the sadder she became. Then as if she didn't believe anything I'd told her, Cora crossed her arms and stuck out her chin. "If Liam's dead, then where is he?" She swept her gaze around the room. "Shouldn't he be here too?"

"I'm afraid that's not how my abilities work," I said. "You're here because I touched your brooch. When Grams found it, she thought it belonged to Liam and believed he'd be the one I summoned."

"Are you saying the only way you can get a ghost to appear is by touching something that belongs to them?" Cora asked.

"As far as I know, yes."

The way Cora tapped her chin and contemplated what I'd said made me nervous. When her gaze met mine again, she asked, "Can you tell me what the dagger looked like?"

"I can do better than that," I said, hopping up and reaching for the flyer in my purse. I placed it on the table in front of her and tapped the picture. "It was this one."

Cora leaned forward, squinted at the image, and gasped. "That dagger belonged to my late husband, Archie." She frowned. "How did it end up in Nadine's shop?"

"That's what I've been wondering," I said. "According to Nadine, it was included in the inventory she acquired when she purchased the store. Do you think Liam sold it to someone?" My instincts disagreed with the possibility. After witnessing Liam's actions, I struggled to believe he was experiencing a bout of seller's remorse. Even more baffling was how he ended up in Cumberpatch in the first place.

"Archie had an entire collection of antique weapons worth a lot of money, which would've gone to Liam after I died. There's no way he would ever get rid of them." Cora tried to pick up the flyer, but her hand went through the table, and she groaned.

"I know," Cora said excitedly, springing to her feet in a fluid, floating motion. After pacing a few steps, she turned and asked, "Do you think you could bring Liam back like you did me?"

"Probably, but I don't think it's such a good idea." The knot in my stomach supported my belief.

"Why not?"

"If my friends and I can't figure out how you died and who ended your life in a limited amount of time, then you won't be able to move on and will be trapped here forever." I pushed out of my chair. "The same rules would apply to Liam, provided he is still here." Which I suspected had a high probability. He hadn't died from natural causes, and I was fairly certain he couldn't cross over until his death was resolved.

"I understand it's a huge responsibility," Cora said. "But what if there's a connection between our deaths, and Liam can provide some answers? Would it be worth it then?"

Only if he actually remembered something that would help us. He'd be a new ghost with fuzzy details about his death. There was a chance he wouldn't recall seeing my friends and me or his interaction with Nadine about the dagger. Since he'd been knifed in the back, the odds were even greater that Liam hadn't seen his killer either.

In order for me to help Cora, I needed her to stick around. Something she might not do if she lost confidence in my abilities. I was afraid to tell her I was still trying to figure out how the magic I'd gotten from the spirit seeker worked. "I've never helped two spirits at the same time, so I'm not sure if it's even possible." I also didn't know if I'd be breaking any magical rules if I tried.

So far, none of my research, which included having Bryce consult the extensive collection of books he owned pertaining to anything paranormal, had provided any useful information regarding the extent of the spirit seeker's powers. Without knowing the limitations of my gift, I shuddered to think what could happen if I purposely summoned more than one spirit. Would it inadvertently open some kind of ghostly floodgate? One that would make my world more chaotic than it already was and cause problems I wouldn't be able to handle?

"But what if it was?" Cora asked, the pleading in her voice hard to resist.

She made a good point. Liam could be the key to solving his and Cora's murders, which would also help

Nadine. "Let's say, hypothetically, that I did agree. I still won't be able to do it because I don't have access to any of Liam's personal items."

"But what if you did?" Cora asked, her smile turning hopeful. "If my brooch and the dagger were in Nadine's shop, then maybe some of our other possessions are there as well?"

"I suppose it's possible." I held up my hand. "Provided they haven't already been sold."

"True, but it's still worth a try, right?" Cora asked.

"I guess so." The trepidation in my voice contradicted the plan already formulating in my mind. "Before I start randomly touching items to see if I can find Liam's ghost, there are some people I need to speak with first."

CHAPTER NINE

I stood on the sidewalk outside the Classic Broom, staring at the door and going over the list of things I wanted to ask Edith and Joyce Haverston. The sisters had a connection to the area's witching community and had done a lot to help me acclimate to having ghostly entities in my life.

I'd waited until after lunch when business in the shop slowed down enough for me to leave with the excuse of running more errands. I shared pretty much everything with Shawna and Jade. The decision not to tell them about my discussion with Cora until after I'd done more research weighed heavy on my mind. I wanted to make sure that going ahead with her request wouldn't somehow unleash a mob of additional spirits or impact those I cared about in a bad way.

"Ready?" I asked, shooting a sidelong glance at Cora and pretending to speak into the cell phone I held near my ear. I'd found it useful for communicating with spirits in public without drawing unwanted attention.

"I think so," Cora said.

I understood her apprehension. It had taken me several visits, and getting to know the Haverstons, before I'd overcome my fear of entering their spooky shop. "It will be all right," I said, reaching for the door handle. "I promise."

Most of the businesses in the neighborhood had a bell hanging over the door. The one inside the shop tinkled as soon as Cora and I stepped inside. The interior was dimly lit, and it took my eyes a few seconds to adjust. After checking to see if there were any customers, and finding none, I slipped my phone back into my purse. I didn't see the sisters either but knew it wouldn't be long before they made an appearance.

"This place isn't creepy at all," Cora mumbled sarcastically. Though she'd adjusted to being a ghost, I didn't get the impression she was into the supernatural or had frequented shops that sold paranormal paraphernalia.

I muffled my chuckle by clearing my throat. Besides being a little mysterious, I believed Joyce and Edith were expert marketers. They knew how to sell their business's magical aspects, making their shop very popular with tourists. Even people who stopped by my family's place raved about the unusual items they'd found during their visits to the Classic Broom.

Cora moved further into the room, perusing the display cases containing shelves filled with a variety of potions. She glanced at me over her shoulder. "Do these really work?"

"I have no idea," I said. "But I wouldn't be surprised if they did."

I'd never had any interest in trying any of the elixirs. When we were younger, and Shawna had gone through a bad breakup, she'd been tempted to try one on her ex-boyfriend. Luckily, Jade and I had succeeded in talking her out of it.

As predicted, Joyce and Edith strolled into the room from a back hallway. "Rylee," they said in unison, then smiled.

"Hey, Joyce, Edith," I said, adding a small hand wave.

Both women were in their forties and had never married. Their crystal blues eyes were the most notable feature on their similar faces. The contrasting color of their waist-length hair; Joyce's a dark brown and Edith's a shiny blonde, was the significant difference between them. Black was the standard color of choice in all their wardrobe selections and enhanced the ominous feel of the place. Today, they were dressed in similar black skirts and matching dark tops. Joyce had a red scarf draped across her shoulders and knotted on one side.

"It's always good to see you," Edith said. "And I sense that you have a new friend." She glanced in Cora's direction, but I knew she couldn't see her ghost.

Edith was the more perceptive of the two, but it was unnerving how the sisters always seemed to know things ahead of time. They'd never openly admitted it, but I was sure they were witches and belonged to a local coven. A coven I hadn't known existed until after I'd asked them for help with my new abilities.

"Yes," I said, sweeping my hand through the air. "This is Cora."

"It's nice to meet you, Cora," Joyce said. "Welcome," Edith said.

"It's a pleasure to meet you too," Cora said, then added, "I think."

The sisters took a little getting used to, so Cora's reaction wasn't unexpected. "She's happy to meet you as well," I told them.

Edith narrowed her eyes as if concentrating on something important, then glanced at Joyce. "I don't think she's a local."

"I agree," Joyce said.

"She's from Brindburrow," I said.

"If she's from out of town, then how did you, um, meet?" Joyce asked. I couldn't tell if the sparkle in her eyes meant she already knew the answer or was hoping for a juicy story.

"Not another cursed object, I hope," Edith said.

"No, it was a brooch from Nadine's shop, courtesy of my grandmother," I said.

Joyce raised her brows. "Awww, tricked you, did she?"

Heat rose on my cheeks, and I shrugged away my embarrassment. "Yeah."

Edith giggled. "Abigail always was a wry one."

"She thought I'd be able to summon…you know," I said, glancing at Cora.

Edith's smile faded, and she asked, "How is Nadine doing?"

"We were going to stop by her old place later today to check on her and see how she's handling her unfortunate incident," Joyce said, glancing at her sister. "Weren't we?"

"Yes." Edith nodded. "I understand you and Logan are the ones who found the body."

News traveled through town faster than a posting on social media. Given their uncanny ability of knowing things, I doubted the sisters relied on gossip to obtain information.

"I assume girlfriends are excluded when it comes to Logan's cases," Joyce said. "But is there a chance he shared any significant details with you?"

Clearly, I wasn't the only one who understood Logan's position on the matter. "Normally, he wouldn't. When I told him about Cora, we discovered that the man who died was her grandson."

"Well," Joyce said, clasping her hands together. "That does sound intriguing."

Edith wrinkled her nose and shot a warning glare at Joyce, then directed her attention toward the spot where Cora was standing. "My sister meant no disrespect, and we are sorry for your loss."

"None taken," Cora said.

"She understands," I said.

"Is this connection to recent events the reason for your visit?" Edith asked.

"It is," I said. "I hate to keep bothering you, but I could use your help."

"It is never a bother," Joyce said. "I take it you haven't heard back about your application for certification yet."

"No," I said, not wanting to discuss my novice status when it came to supernatural sleuthing in front of Cora.

Edith tsked. "Don't worry. I'm sure you'll be hearing from them shortly."

"I do believe you're right," Joyce said, smiling at her sister. "Now, what can we help you with?"

I spent the next five minutes telling the sisters everything I knew about Liam's murder and his interest in the dagger. "Cora thinks if I tried to summon Liam, he might have information that could help both of them." I inhaled a calming breath. "I've never dealt with more than one spirit at a time. I'm afraid it might not work, or if it does, that I'll end up summoning additional spirits."

"Hmm," Joyce said, tapping her chin. "That is quite a dilemma."

"And understandably disconcerting at the same time," Edith said. "Knowing there are ghosts in the world is one thing, but not being able to see them is different than having them popping in and out of your life on a daily basis…possibly forever."

"That's why I came to you," I said. "You've been wonderful about helping me in the past, and I was hoping you might know the answer or be able to point me in the direction of someone who does."

"I'm afraid my knowledge on summoning is limited, so no," Joyce said, turning to Edith. "You?"

"No, I can't say I do either," Edith said. She contemplatively gazed at the floor for a few seconds before adding, "There is someone who might know or at least be able to give you some guidance."

"Who?" I asked, trying not to sound overly excited.

"That sounds promising," Cora said from across the room. She'd gone back to wandering around the store, examining some of the contents on shelves and in display cases.

"Do you remember Deeann Dufner?" Edith asked.

"Of course," I said. I didn't think I'd ever forget the woman who possessed necromancer abilities. She'd been extremely helpful in my quest to reunite Martin's ghost with his mate Pete.

"I think we should give her a call," Edith said, slipping her cell phone out of the pocket of her skirt and giving the screen a swipe.

"Good morning, Deeann," Edith said, then smiled at the response she'd received from the other end of the call. A few seconds later, she lowered the phone and tapped the screen. "I hope you don't mind, but I have you on speaker with Joyce and Rylee. We also have a visitor named Cora who won't be able to participate vocally but is listening in."

Cora grinned at Edith's thoughtfulness.

"Not at all," Deeann said. She also knew about my abilities and must've picked up that Cora was a ghost because she didn't ask any additional questions about her. "What can I do for you today?"

Edith gave me a nod, urging me to explain my situation. "Hi, Deeann," I said. "It's Rylee."

"It's so good to hear from you," she said. "I hope things are going well with your...adventures."

"I have to admit they aren't easy and rarely go smoothly, but they definitely aren't boring," I said.

Deeann giggled. "I understand, so what can I help you with?"

"To solve my current 'adventure', it has been suggested that I summon an additional spirit." I glanced at Cora and gave her a reassuring smile.

"I see," Deeann said.

"Did you hear about the body they found at The Booty Bazaar?" I asked.

"I did. Such an awful thing to happen to Nadine,"

Deeann said. Given their professions, I wasn't surprised the two women knew each other.

Out of nervous habit, I tucked a brown strand behind my ear. "The man who died is Cora's grandson." Rather than risk customers showing up and interrupting a lengthy explanation of how I'd ended up with Cora instead of Liam, I said, "It's a long and complicated story, one I'll be happy to share with you some other time."

"That's not a problem," Deeann said, then added, "Go on."

"Given the parameters of my abilities, do you think it's possible to summon an additional spirit without opening a larger gateway?" I winced, thinking about the catastrophic possibilities.

I assumed Deeann was pondering my question since she didn't answer immediately.

I possessed limited patience, but in this instance, Joyce seemed anxious for an answer. "Deeann, are you still there?"

"Sorry, yes," Deeann said. "Rylee, all magic is governed by rules. Since none of us are clear what they are for your unique capabilities, I don't know for sure what would happen if you tried to summon another ghost."

"Well, thanks anyway," I said. "It was worth a try."

"I'd still like to help if I can," Deeann said. "If you don't mind waiting a few hours before making a decision, there are some books in my personal library I'd like to look through first."

"That would be great," I said.

"Good, then I'll call you and let you know if I find anything," Deeann said. "Joyce, Edith, it was good talking to you."

As soon as she disconnected the call, Edith slipped the phone back into her pocket. "You'll be sure to let us know what she finds out, won't you?"

"Yes," I said. "And thanks again for all your help."

"It was our pleasure," Joyce said.

The front door opened before I reached it, and a young man and woman who looked like they were in their early twenties stepped inside. The guy gave the interior a skeptical glance, then whispered something into the woman's ear before taking a backward step toward the exit. Apparently, he wasn't thrilled about the place's scary vibe.

"Welcome," Joyce said to the couple. "If there's anything I can help you with, please don't hesitate to ask."

"Thanks, I will," the woman said, latching onto the guy's arm and dragging him into the store.

I looked in Cora's direction and was disappointed to see that she'd disappeared, most likely startled by the couple's arrival.

The last time I was here, Edith followed me to the door and offered me some words of wisdom that made no sense at the time. I'd made it as far as the sidewalk thinking I'd escape without receiving an undecipherable clue, then cringed when she called out my name. "Yes," I said, forcing a smile as I turned.

"A discovery from the past will bring clarity to the future."

And just like all my previous visits, she spun and closed the door before I could ask her what she meant.

CHAPTER TEN

After a long, exhausting day, I was tempted to go to bed early. Instead, I pulled out my laptop, hoping to do some online research into Cora's death. I'd just changed out of my work clothes and into a baggy T-shirt and comfortable pair of sweats when I heard a knock on the door.

I hadn't been expecting visitors and was surprised to find Shawna and Jade standing outside, similarly dressed in dark jackets and jeans. The only difference in their attire was the worn lime green backpack Shawna had hitched on her shoulder. A bag she'd gotten when she was twelve years old and had used to carry her books all the way through high school.

Besides dropping by without calling first, the fact that they never coordinated their clothing was my first clue that something was amiss. "Change in plans," Shawna said as she urged Jade inside, then surveyed the area behind the building as if they'd been followed.

"Change in what plans?" I asked, closing the door. The last time Jade and I had talked, I'd shared Cora's idea and what little I'd learned from my trip to the Classic Broom. Other than promising to share the information with

Shawna, we hadn't discussed doing anything else.

After that, I'd spent a busy afternoon taking care of customers in the shop and hoping I'd hear back from Deeann, which I hadn't.

"Helping Cora, of course," Shawna said, dropping her backpack on the floor, then plopping down on the couch. She reached over and pulled Barley from his favorite spot onto her lap.

"While we were discussing the situation, we realized we didn't have any suspects for Cora's death," Jade said as she settled into a kitchen chair across from where I'd been sitting.

Shawna cleared her throat.

Jade rolled her eyes. "Okay, Shawna's the one who figured it out."

"Thank you," Shawna said smugly.

"And," Jade drew out the word. "Since time is of the essence, and we can't rely on Logan giving us information—"

Shawna interrupted by saying, "Which I think is wrong. Having a detective for a boyfriend should entitle you to special treatment."

Those kinds of expectations had been known to strain relationships, even wreck them. "It's because of our relationship that I don't want 'special treatment'," I said. Though, given the current circumstances, we could definitely use anything Logan uncovered. "I also don't want him to risk losing his job because he shared information he shouldn't have."

Roy was a good sheriff with lots of integrity. I didn't think he'd let his family tie with Logan influence his decisions.

"Oh," Shawna said. "I hadn't thought of that."

Other than a text to say "Hello" and see how my day was going, I hadn't gotten an invite from Logan to have the talk he'd mentioned. Rather than add to my anxiety by discussing it further, I returned to my seat and changed the subject. "Getting back to what you were saying," I said to Jade.

"Right." She propped her elbows on the table. "Have you heard back from Deeann yet?"

"No," I said.

"That's okay," Shawna said. "We can still move forward with our plan."

Frustrated, I threw my hands up in the air. "What plan?"

"The one where we sneak into Nadine's shop, borrow her ledger, and anything that might have belonged to Liam," Jade said.

"That way," Shawna said. "You're ready to go when she calls and tells you it's okay to summon his spirit."

"If," I said, emphasizing the word. "She says it's all right."

Shawna tsked. "She will. I know it." She set Barley aside, eliciting a disgruntled kitty noise, then walked over to join Jade and me. "I did some online research and found something interesting about Cora."

"You did?" I asked.

"Uh-huh." Shawna pointed at my laptop. "Do you want me to show you?"

"Sure," I said, then moved to the empty chair on my right so she could sit down.

Shawna skimmed her fingers across the keys. "It's a six-month-old article from the local newspaper in Brindburrow." She turned the computer, so the screen was facing me. "After seeing this, I think you'll agree with our plan."

The report on Cora's death had been condensed into three paragraphs and didn't take me long to read. The local police were convinced she'd interrupted someone breaking into her home, which aligned with what Cora had told me. The article noted that some items had been stolen but didn't mention anything specific.

Once I finished, I looked up and found my friends

staring at me expectantly. "You think the brooch and the dagger were taken during the robbery," I said.

"Don't you?" Shawna asked.

"Possibly," I said. Cora couldn't recall the details of her death and wouldn't be able to tell us what went missing. Liam, as her surviving heir, would most likely know. Or at least he would've if he was still alive.

"I know you're worried about what could happen if you summon Liam," Jade said. "If we find an answer in the ledger, then you won't need to."

Maybe my friends were right. I wanted to help Liam but needed to know what I'd be risking by summoning him first. Solving Cora's murder took precedence, even if it meant sneaking into a crime scene, something that continued to be a part of our sleuthing routine.

"What ledger?" Cora said, appearing in the kitchen next to the sink. Her hair was done in a single braid, and she wore casual slacks instead of a long skirt.

"Hey, Cora," I said.

"She's here?" Shawna asked excitedly. "Having her go with us will help out tremendously."

"Rylee," Cora said. "What is she talking about?"

"They, I mean we, have a plan," I said. Now that Cora was here, I felt more confident about being successful. I spent the next few minutes providing her with an explanation, which included showing her the article on the laptop screen.

"What if we find more of Archie's collection in Nadine's shop?" Cora asked. "Are we going to take those as well?"

After repeating what she said, I contemplated whether or not removing additional items from the crime scene was a good idea.

"Technically, the dagger and any of the antiques that belonged to Cora's husband would've become Liam's possessions after his death. So you should be able to use any of them to summon him," Shawna said with the confidence of a supernatural expert. She wasn't any more knowledgeable than I was, but her reasoning had merit.

"Are you sure Liam's grandfather died from natural causes?" Jade asked. "We don't need any unexpected manifestations."

I appreciated my friend's support. I didn't need or want another unplanned ghost either.

"Quite certain," Cora huffed.

"She's sure," I said.

"Okay then," Shawna said, grinning as she pushed out of her chair. "Let's get this covert mission underway."

CHAPTER ELEVEN

After changing into an outfit that closely matched Jade's and Shawna's, we headed for Nadine's new shop. It was early in the evening, but the sun had disappeared some time ago, and there was a crisp chill in the air. Shawna was convinced we needed to use the alleys and shadows along the sides of buildings to avoid being seen by anyone who might recognize us.

I didn't think it was necessary. Any tourists we encountered wouldn't know us, and it wasn't like any of the locals would care if we were out walking. There was also no way to hide her backpack, which seemed to glow in the dark. Our trip, which normally would've taken five minutes if we'd used the sidewalks, had turned into twenty.

I'd vetoed the idea of contacting Nadine to go along with us. Until she was cleared from being a suspect, something I wouldn't know until I spoke with Logan again, I didn't want her to be involved in what Shawna deemed our 'covert mission', not if there was a chance Shawna, Jade, and I might get caught.

I hadn't even told Grams what we were doing because I knew she'd want to come along. After her debacle with the brooch, she wasn't exactly on Logan's good side. I had a feeling if he found out she was doing something else, he might not be so lenient.

"Are you sure about this?" Jade asked as she tucked her hands in her jacket pockets and nervously stared at the rear door of the building.

I wished if she was going to have second thoughts, she'd done it while we were still in my warm apartment. If the police in Brindburrow had found Cora's attacker, I wouldn't have been able to summon her. We could still turn back, but it wouldn't get us any closer to solving her murder.

I stared at the police tape crisscrossing the door. The shudder I felt wasn't entirely caused by the cold. "No, but what choice do we have?" I asked. There was no way Logan would voluntarily let us inside. If I shared my suspicions about the ledger, he might confiscate it as evidence without letting me read through the pages.

"Exactly," Shawna said. Her determination to complete our task hadn't wavered in the slightest.

"What if we find something useful in the ledger, but it's no longer in the shop?" Jade asked. "Are you going to visit the buyers and ask to see their purchases?"

"If the possession part of ghost summoning is accurate, then it wouldn't do any good," Shawna said. "The buyer would be the new owner, and the thing they bought would no longer be linked to Liam."

"She's right," I said. "Why don't we worry about the "what ifs" until after we get a peek at the ledger." Maybe we'd get lucky, and the seller's name would be listed.

Cora stood a few feet away from me. She shifted back and forth on her feet, no doubt worried that we'd change our minds. I wanted to reassure her and said, "While I'm checking Nadine's office, Cora can look through the store and see if she recognizes anything."

"Just to be clear," I said, tapping Shawna's arm. "This is an in-and-out mission. No lingering or taking additional trinkets."

"Geez," Shawna groaned. "Help Grams one time, and I'm marked for life."

"Yeah, right," Jade said, a reminder that Shawna had been my grandmother's co-conspirator more than a few times over the years. Most of them with similar results.

Before the direction of our conversation turned into a debate, I asked, "Are you sure you can get us inside?" It was too bad Cora was a new ghost. If she'd been in our realm a lot longer, she might have acquired the ability to move things and could've slipped through the wall and opened the door from the inside.

"Absolutely," Shawna said as she slipped the backpack off her shoulder. "I've been practicing with the lock pick set I bought for you."

I'd appreciated the gesture but had refused the gift since I had no interest in learning the skill. I was happy to let Shawna take over as the group's expert, though at the time, I'd hoped it wouldn't be a necessity.

Shawna interlocked her fingers and cracked her knuckles. "I've gotten much better since the last time I used them." She pulled a small flashlight out of her bag, then handed it to Jade, who clicked it on and aimed it at the lock above the door's handle.

"Do you do this often?" Cora asked.

"No, I prefer doing things that won't get us into trouble," I said.

Shawna was busy concentrating on the lock. Jade glanced in my direction, acknowledging that she knew I was talking to Cora, then added, "Though most of the time, it doesn't work out that way."

A few seconds later, a click echoed through the silence, followed by a squeal from Shawna.

"Shawna," Jade said. "Covert means not letting everyone in the neighborhood know we're here."

"Sorry," she said, getting to her feet. She twisted the handle, but the door didn't open. After giving it a harder tug, Shawna asked, "Do you think it's wedged shut?"

"No, it has a security lock, which I'm pretty sure you won't be able to open with those picks," Nadine said as she stepped out of the shadows, making us all squeal louder than Shawna had. I wondered if she'd tiptoed the entire length of the alley because I hadn't heard any footsteps.

"Hey, girls," Grams said, grinning at Nadine as she stepped around her. "Told you they'd be here."

Trying to be stealthy in a hot pink sweat suit was no better than Shawna toting around a neon backpack. Since my attempts to keep my grandmother from involving herself in my ghostly missions continually failed, we'd need to have a serious discussion about her wardrobe choice. At least Nadine had enough sense to wear dark clothing.

I glanced to where I'd last seen Cora, hoping the commotion hadn't frightened her off again. She had her hand clasped over her mouth, amusement sparkling in her eyes. Clearly, I wasn't enjoying the jolt to my nervous system as much as she was.

"Grams, what are you doing here?" I asked through gritted teeth.

She slapped her hands on her hips. "Same as you…searching for clues."

"We were looking for something that might help Rylee summon Liam," Shawna said.

"Even better," Grams said.

I shook my head, wishing I'd sworn my friends to secrecy before leaving my place. To prevent Grams from encouraging Shawna to join her in doing something that would lead to trouble, I said, "Actually, we came for the ledger. I'm not summoning Liam until I hear back from Deeann."

"Are you talking about Deeann Dufner?" Nadine asked.

"Yes," I said.

"What does she have to do with this?" Grams asked.

"Cora thought bringing back Liam might help solve her

murder, and I agree," I said, smiling at the ghost. Even if our efforts proved moot, it was a good idea, and I thought she deserved the credit. "I wasn't sure what would happen if I summoned another ghost, so I went to see the Haverston sisters, who suggested I talk to Deeann. She didn't know either but offered to see what she could find out."

"That was a wise decision," Nadine said. "If you don't understand the rules governing the supernatural, all kinds of things could go wrong."

Getting praising words from Nadine meant a lot and made me feel better about my decision.

"I think you should know that Logan made sure everything on the floor near the body had been bagged up," Nadine said. "So I don't know if we'll find anything."

"There might still be something in the display case," I said. "Cora's here, and she's going to help." I hitched a thumb in her direction in case Nadine and Grams wanted to talk to her. I'd have to repeat her replies, but it would keep Cora from feeling ignored.

"Good," Nadine said, glancing in Cora's direction. "If you find anything that belonged to your grandson, we'll take it with us."

"I don't think you should get involved," I said. "Maybe you and Grams should leave. You could get into a lot of trouble if anyone finds out you were here." Explaining why wasn't necessary.

"No more than the three of you," Nadine said. "Besides, that poor man was murdered in my shop, and I'm not going to sit around while you put yourselves in danger to find his killer."

After remembering what it was like to be on Logan's suspect list, I couldn't argue with her logic. The man had a way of making people squirm, even if they were innocent.

Nadine held out her hand to Jade. "Can I borrow your flashlight?" She aimed it at the wall next to the door frame, then started patting the exterior. "Here it is."

I had no idea what she was talking about until she pulled on the edge of a brick, which turned out to be a panel camouflaged to look like the rest of the wall and hid a numbered keypad. "That's pretty ingenious," I said.

"Even in daylight, it's hard to spot unless you know what you're looking for," Nadine said.

"Nathan has his own business in Portland. After he took over things for Hildie, rather than figure out a way to keep both places open, he decided it would be easier to close her shop. Since some of her inventory is worth a lot of money, he didn't want to risk a break-in and had the extra security installed."

"It didn't stop someone from going in through the front though, did it?" Shawna said.

"He thought the traffic and lights on the street would act as a deterrent," Nadine said. "Nathan was more worried about the alley because it's not well-lit and easier to access without being seen."

"Seems he was right about that," Grams said, eying my friends and me.

Pointing out that we weren't the only ones sneaking around would be moot, so I didn't bother.

"So, what's the plan?" Nadine asked me. She tapped a sequence of numbers, and another lock in the door clicked.

"I'd like to take a look around," I said. "And now that you're here, would you mind showing us Hildie's ledger?" I asked.

"Not at all," Nadine said, handing the flashlight back to Jade. "In case something goes wrong, I don't want everyone to get in trouble on my account. I think you, me, and Cora should be the only ones that go inside."

Surprisingly, Grams spoke up before anyone could voice their objections to the plan. "Nadine's right. It won't do any good if we all end up in jail. Besides, my eyesight's not as good as it used to be, and I could use your help."

We all knew my grandmother wasn't a frail old lady and

could see just fine.

Shawna snorted. "Sure, okay. I guess we can stay out here and help you be a lookout."

Since I had a flashlight, Nadine let me duck under the tape and go first. Cora could've easily walked through the wall; instead, she followed us through the open doorway.

I glanced down the hallway leading to the front of the building, noting that the lampposts outside cast enough light through the windows to see where I was going. There was a chance that someone might walk or drive by and notice thin beams of light bouncing around the interior. "Why don't you go get the ledger," I said, handing the flashlight to Nadine. "I'll go up front with Cora and look around."

"Sounds good to me," Nadine said, heading for a closed door on the right, which I assumed must be the office.

The shop looked pretty much the same as it had the night Logan and I found Liam's body. The glass shards had been cleaned off the floor, and the wooden board used to replace the damage on the door was securely in place.

I moved toward the display case housing antique weapons and closest to the place where the death had occurred. It didn't take a genius to know that the dark area staining the wooden floor was dried blood. "Cora," I said when she stopped to stare at the spot where Liam's body had been.

She shook her head as if coming out of a trance, then mumbled, "Yes."

I pointed at the shelves. "Do you see anything that might help?"

Cora peered through the glass, then checked the adjacent case, frowning as she went. "I don't see anything."

If there had been more items from Archie's collection on the shelves, were they already sold, or were they taken during the break-in?

"I've got it," Nadine said, holding up the ledger as she quietly entered the room.

"Great," I said. "Hopefully, we'll find answers to some of our questions."

"Any luck out here?" she asked.

"Nothing so far."

Shawna appeared in the doorway, the beam from her flashlight hitting me in the face. "Guys," she said in a panicked voice. "We need to go. *Now*." A few seconds later, Jade and Grams burst into the room after her.

Cora squeaked, then disappeared. Nadine jumped and tossed the ledger, which sailed through the air and landed on the floor a few feet away.

"What happened?" I asked, snatching the flashlight from my friend and switching it off.

"It's the coppers," Grams said, brushing past me on her way to the front door.

"I think Roy has Elliott out patrolling on foot," Jade said.

"Did he see you?" Nadine asked, retrieving the ledger off the floor.

"I don't think so, which is why we need to…" Jade swept her hand through the air, then hurried after Grams.

"Go," Shawna said, tugging the sleeve of my jacket.

Once we were all outside, Nadine stopped to pull a set of keys out of her pocket and insert them into the door's lock. A metallic click rang through the air at the same time the sound of footsteps came from the corner of the building.

"Hurry," Shawna said.

My racing pulse and the fear of getting caught were all the motivations I needed to move as if my life depended on winning a race.

CHAPTER TWELVE

Talk about a frightful and exhilarating night. Even avoiding the main street, our group reached my apartment in record time. My heart was still pounding after our narrow escape from Nadine's shop.

Everyone but me had collapsed on the furniture in the living room. I leaned against the kitchen counter, trying to normalize my breathing.

"Is this what it's like every time you investigate on a ghost's behalf?" Nadine asked, her hand pressed to her chest.

"Pretty much," I said, bending over to scratch Barley's head. He must've been sleeping in the bedroom because he'd padded into the room shortly after we'd arrived and rubbed against my leg. After realizing he wouldn't get any snacks, he curled up on the couch next to Shawna.

"Except for the times when Rylee decided to face off with a killer," Jade said.

Nadine widened her blue eyes. "You did, really?"

"I didn't do it intentionally," I said. "It just seems to happen." A lot.

I wasn't going to share that concern, not when I needed to remain focused on my current dilemma. Our attempt to find something that belonged to Liam might not have been successful, but at least we'd gotten the ledger. Thinking about Liam reminded me that I still hadn't heard back from Deeann. I'd muted the ringer on my phone before Shawna, Jade, and I had headed out. I slipped it out of my jacket pocket, reset the volume, then checked my messages.

"Anything from Deeann?" Grams asked.

"No," I said, frowning at the screen. There was, however, a text from Logan asking about my day. Seeing the emoji of a smiling face helped lighten my frustration. He'd also tried calling a half hour after sending the text, no doubt because I hadn't replied to his message, something that rarely happened.

He might like to be in charge when it came to his job, but he wasn't a controlling boyfriend. His work had shown him the dark side of humanity, so I knew his call was based on concern for my welfare.

I wasn't a master at disguising my emotions, not after our near miss with being caught, so calling him right now wasn't an option. I quickly typed in a response, "Everything's fine. Talk to you tomorrow."

Once my breathing returned to normal, I went to the refrigerator and pulled out enough bottles of water for everyone. Nadine was already leafing through the ledger. After settling into the kitchen chair I'd scooted closer to the group, I took a long swallow, then asked, "Find anything?"

She pointed to a line on the page. "This could be the dagger Liam was asking about."

"Is there any additional information?" I asked.

"Only a date, a brief description, and an amount which I assume was the purchase price," Nadine said. She leaned forward and turned the ledger around so I could see the page.

Was the seller's name omitted because the items were obtained by less than legal means? I thought about Hildie and her association with Jake Durant, who, up until his death, had caused all kinds of problems for my Uncle Max. Was it possible Jake had gotten Hildie involved in some of his shady dealings?

Tying the dagger back to the person Hildie had bought it from would've been helpful. It didn't necessarily mean they were the killer. Jake was connected to people in Cumberpatch, and since there wasn't a location listed either, it could easily be someone who lived locally. Maybe even a tourist who visited frequently. Without the additional information I'd been hoping for, I didn't have anyone to question or add to my non-existent suspect list.

"I could take this home and compare it to the computer database for the shop," Nadine said. "Unless you'd like me to leave it with you."

"If all the information is like this," I said, glancing at the open page. "I don't think I'll find anything useful. If you don't mind, a comparison would be great."

"I don't mind," Nadine said. "My old shop is still open, so I can start looking between appointments."

We spent the next few minutes contemplating and sipping our drinks. Shawna broke the silence by asking, "Has Cora reappeared yet?"

I hadn't felt a drop in temperature, but I glanced behind me anyway. "Not yet. Why?"

"I wanted to ask her if she had any relatives living in the area," she said.

"I don't think she does," I said. "I could be wrong, but I got the impression that Liam was her only living relative."

"If Liam lived in Brindburrow and didn't have any friends or family here, at least not that we know of, then he would've needed a place to stay, right?" Shawna asked. "How much do you want to bet he had a room at the Beaumont Inn?"

"Please tell us you're not suggesting we break into his room next," Jade said, snatching Barley off the couch and pulling him onto her lap. After a few seconds of scratching the top of his head, he closed his eyes and started purring. My cat had a calming effect on anyone who came in contact with him. Whether they realized it or not, my friends used his special talent whenever they were stressed.

Before she could answer, I said, "I don't think it would be helpful. Logan's efficient and thorough. He's probably already removed all of Liam's belongings."

"I was thinking more along the lines of gossip recon," Shawna said. "Maybe we could gather clues by talking to some of the staff."

"What happens if Lavender's hanging around?" Jade asked. "We aren't exactly on her friend list, and she'll be suspicious if we all show up and start asking her employees questions."

My stomach knotted at the thought of purposely putting myself on Lavender's radar. We'd had history since high school, and not the good kind. She went out of her way to be a pain in my backside every chance she got.

Fortunately for me, the inn was located near the coast, and Lavender avoided shopping in my family's shop. The only time our paths crossed was at community events or if we worked on a committee together.

If any of my relatives knew the reason the Abbotts and Spencers didn't get along, they'd refused to share or confirm my speculations. I was certain it had something to do with our grandmothers and possibly my deceased grandfather, but I'd never been able to coerce Grams into telling me what had happened.

My parents had been around a lot longer than me, and I didn't think they knew any details either.

"She might not have a problem if Rylee and I showed up with more of Nadine's flyers," Shawna said.

I snorted. "There's no way Lavender will ever be okay with me showing up at her family's inn." Though, technically, she only managed the place. Her sister Serena was half-owner because she'd married Colin Beaumont.

Besides being wealthy and handsome, his family had owned the place for years.

Shawna ignored my comment. "Molly Jacobs works there, and she chats with the guests all the time. Maybe Liam shared something important with her. Like why he was visiting Cumberpatch. If you can get Cora to go with us, she can zip around and see if any of Liam's things are still there."

Keeping up with Shawna was difficult, but sometimes her logic made sense. This was one of those times when she might be onto something. I never understood how Molly could stand to spend so much time with my nemesis. On the other hand, Molly was friendly and actively participated in the town's mainstream gossip line. Liam also had one of Nadine's flyers when he came into the shop. Maybe he'd picked it up while staying at the inn.

"I work the dinner shift, so we could go tomorrow morning," Shawna said. "If you can get away."

"Of course, she can," Grams said.

A musical tune emanating from my phone filled the air. I rushed into the kitchen and puffed a relieved sigh when I saw Deeann's name on the screen. "Hey, Deeann."

"It's not too late to call, is it?" she asked.

"No, not at all." She could've called at midnight, and I wouldn't have been upset.

"Oh, good." She must've been calling from home because I could hear children giggling in the background. "I couldn't find anything in my books, so I reached out to some of my more knowledgeable friends." Before I could panic, she hurried to say, "I want you to know that I didn't mention your name, only your abilities."

"I appreciate that." I still wasn't ready for everyone in town to know what I could do. As it was, courtesy of Lavender, quite a few people thought I was a witch. Another reason I wasn't looking forward to visiting the inn.

"Do you remember me telling you there were rules

when dealing with the supernatural?" Deeann asked.

"Yes," I said.

"According to my sources, they believe the rules that apply to one encounter should work for any additional ghosts you want to summon." She paused. "There are no absolutes, and I can't guarantee that the information is one hundred percent accurate, but I think you should be able to move forward without drastic ramifications."

"Thanks, Deeann," I said.

"No problem," she said, disconnecting the call.

"Well?" Grams asked.

"She doesn't think it will be a problem, but I'm only going to do it if we're absolutely sure the item belongs to Liam. No trial and error." I glared at Grams, then Shawna. "Agreed?"

Both women nodded; their smug and unnerving grins added to my anxiety.

CHAPTER THIRTEEN

The next morning after I'd gotten Barley and myself ready for work, I opened the apartment door and found Logan with his hand raised, ready to knock. My stomach fluttered like it always did when I saw him. Mainly because he was such a handsome guy.

The world around me always seemed to disappear when he smiled and looked at me as if I was the only thing that mattered to him. "Logan, what are you doing here?" I managed to ask in an even, non-crackly voice.

His dark brown hair was usually neatly combed, but today the strands were mussed as if he'd run his hand through them numerous times. Something he usually did when he was frustrated.

"Would you like to come inside?" I asked, taking a step back to let him enter.

"Not if it makes you late for work," he said.

I grinned at his thoughtfulness, even if it wasn't necessary. I was in charge and didn't have to clock my time. "Grams won't mind after I tell her I was with you." My grandmother thought Logan was awesome, something I agreed with. She encouraged the time we spent together.

Barley meowed and squirmed. "Here, let me," he said,

taking him from my arms. Logan was one of my cat's favorite people. Barley settled into his arms and started purring without receiving any head scratchings first.

"Is everything okay?" Logan asked. "With us, I mean."

"Yes," I said. He rarely demonstrated self-doubt about anything, our relationship included, so I was confused. "Why wouldn't it be?"

"You weren't answering your phone last night," Logan said. "I was worried and decided to stop by and make sure you were all right."

"Didn't you receive my text?" I asked, sure I'd pressed the send button. I'd thought my message would suffice, but it seemed I'd been wrong. I hated bending the truth but couldn't tell him I'd had the ringer muted when he called or why. I'd planned to reach out after I got to work and had one of Mattie's tasty coffees from her shop across the street. Clearly, that hadn't been the right decision.

"I did." He searched my eyes with his intense gaze. "But it was cryptic and didn't have any kitty emojis."

I had a favorite emoji that I often used in my texts, but because I'd been in a hurry, I hadn't thought to add it. I should've known he'd pick up on anything out of the ordinary but hadn't considered how it would be interpreted. "Can you stay?"

"Yes," Logan said.

"Maybe now's a good time to have that discussion you mentioned in your office," I said. After unclipping Barley's leash, I slipped the strap off my shoulder and set my purse on the table.

Logan placed my cat on the floor, then took my hand and led me to the couch. Once we were seated, he shifted sideways and asked, "Have you had any luck helping Cora?"

"No. Shawna thinks Liam might have been staying at the Beaumont Inn, so we're taking a trip out there this morning."

"If you're after Liam's belongings, I already collected

them," Logan said.

"I told her as much." I was proud that I knew him so well. "We plan to deliver flyers for Nadine so we can chat with employees." It felt good to be helping Nadine with her advertising, but the trip could still be a waste of time. Even so, we desperately needed clues, and I was willing to risk an unpleasant encounter with Lavender to find one.

Logan raised a brow. "Do you have a possible suspect, someone I should be questioning?"

"No, it's just that people in town like to gossip and are more willing to share juicy tidbits if they don't realize they're being investigated."

He chuckled. "Is that a nice way of saying I'm intimidating?"

I shrugged. "Not to me, but to others…"

"I guess I'll have to work on that," he said.

I placed my hand over his. "Personally, I wouldn't change a thing."

Not many people could embarrass Logan. It was exhilarating to know I was one of the few who could make him blush.

"How about you?" I asked. "Have you made any progress with Liam's investigation?"

"Not much, I'm afraid," he said. "Though I can tell you I've ruled out Nadine."

"Well, that's good to know." I smiled. "Have you told Nadine yet?"

"I plan to call her after I leave here."

"Does that mean you're also releasing the crime scene?" Thanks to the numerous hours I'd spent watching mystery shows with Shawna and Jade, I'd gotten good at police terminology. Having a detective for a boyfriend hadn't hurt either.

"Yes," he said with a grin that showcased his dimples. "She'll be able to open again tomorrow."

It was a relief to hear that Nadine was no longer a suspect. I was still convinced that Cora's and Liam's deaths were connected, so I wasn't going to stop trying to solve their murders.

"For obvious reasons, we've never discussed collaborating in the past," Logan said. "But given the recent circumstances, maybe we should reevaluate the dynamics."

"Are you suggesting we bend the rules?" I wanted clarification before I agreed to move forward.

"More like adjust them to fit the situation," Logan said. "And given your new ability, I have a feeling your encounters will overlap with future cases."

I didn't want to think about the deaths I might witness in the future, but having Logan's assistance would help tremendously.

"Is it my imagination, or is it getting cold in here?" Logan asked.

I hadn't removed my jacket, but now that he'd brought it to my attention, I could feel a chill on my face and hands. A few seconds later, Cora appeared in the middle of my living room. She was back to wearing a mid-length skirt but had switched her top to a long-sleeve, lightweight sweater.

"Um, we have company," I said, tipping my head toward Cora.

"Who's this?" Cora asked, fluffing the bun at her nape and giving Logan an appreciative smile. A woman's age didn't matter when it came to my boyfriend. They all found him as good-looking as I did, even after they were dead.

"Cora," I said. "This is Logan, the detective I was telling you about."

"The boyfriend, right?" I detected a hint of disappointment in her voice.

I nodded.

"Hello, Cora," Logan said.

"He can't see me either, can he?" Cora asked.

"No, but if you have any questions, I'll be happy to

pass them along."

"Do you think he can help us find something that belonged to Liam, so you can do your thing?" she asked.

I repeated what she'd asked to Logan.

"I think so," he said.

I hoped Cora's sniffle didn't turn into a ghostly version of sobbing.

"What did you have in mind?" I asked.

"I can't remove evidence from the station," Logan said. "That doesn't mean my girlfriend can't stop by for a visit and accidentally touch something that belonged to Liam." I wondered if sifting through Liam's things would also include sharing any information Logan had uncovered about Liam's and Cora's deaths. I decided to save that question for later when I could negotiate without a ghost in the room.

As soon as the words "It's a date" left my mouth, a melodic tune erupted from Logan's jacket pocket. He looked at the screen on his phone and got to his feet. "Duty calls." He leaned over and kissed me. It wasn't long and lingering, but it wasn't chaste either. It did, however, take my breath away and had me looking forward to our semi-date that evening.

CHAPTER FOURTEEN

By the time I'd dropped Barley off and returned with a steaming cup of French Vanilla coffee and a delectable cream cheese muffin from across the street, Shawna had arrived and was leaning on the back counter, perusing a copy of the *Swashbuckler Gazette*.

With her hair down, the blue streaks were more noticeable. I was used to seeing her in her uniform when she stopped by the shop. Since she wasn't scheduled to work until much later, she'd dressed in a nice shirt and jeans.

I wasn't interested in hearing my horoscope for the day and was glad to see that she'd already moved on from her favorite page and was reading through the headlines section. "Anything interesting?" I asked. Sometimes Troy did a follow-up article for the unnaturally deceased if he gleaned new information.

"Huh-uh," Shawna said and kept reading.

I took a sip of my coffee and waited for Grams and Jade to finish helping their customers, then proceeded to tell everyone about my discussion with Logan.

Shawna looked up from whatever she was reading and asked, "You haven't changed your mind about going to the inn, have you? Because I still think it's a good idea. Especially if your secret rendezvous with Logan at the station later today doesn't work."

"Why wouldn't it work?" Grams asked after giving Shawna a friendly nudge so she'd make room for her to scoot in next to her. Reading the paper was something the women often did.

"Oh, I don't know," I said. "Maybe because I don't know the full extent of my abilities, and they tend to do the unexpected."

"That's true," Jade said.

Shawna scowled. "Have you told Cora yet?"

"She was there when Logan and I talked about it and promised to be there when I tried," I said. I couldn't blame her. I didn't know how the afterlife worked. If the summoning was successful, it might be the only time she got to see her grandson again.

"Is she here now?" Shawna asked. "And is she planning to go with us to the inn?"

"No to both," I said. "Since Liam's belongings are at the police station, it doesn't make sense for her to travel with us." It usually only took a few days for new ghosts to gain some control over where they went. Now that Cora wasn't trapped in her home, she was probably testing her freedom and exploring Cumberpatch.

"Well, darn," Shawna said. "It would've been nice to have her along if we needed some ghostly recon."

"Other than valuable information, I don't think there's anything else inside the building that will help with our investigation," I said.

"It never hurts to be prepared," Shawna said.

No, it didn't, but I was willing to bet we'd be okay without Cora.

My muffin's enticing aroma was calling to me, and apparently, Barley as well since he'd come out of hiding to rub against my leg. Before I could silence my rumbling stomach, I needed to take care of business first and asked,

"Has Nadine been by yet?"

"Yes," Grams said, reaching under the counter to retrieve a stack of sales flyers. "She dropped these off and said she'd call you once she had a chance to compare the ledger with the information on her computer."

"Wonderful," I said, holding up my bag. "I'm going back to eat my breakfast, then we can go."

***

Since Shawna was great at recognizing voices, she called the inn first to make sure Molly was working. It might have been a little rude to hang up as soon as our friend answered, but at least we had verification our trip wouldn't be wasted and avoided giving Lavender a heads-up.

The two-lane road on the edge of town wound its way along the bay and overlooked the ocean. The area was sparsely populated, but the breathtaking landscape made up for the lack of homes. The trees, grass, and foliage showed off a variety of vibrant greens. It wouldn't be long before wildflower blooms added bright reds, yellows, and purple to the scenery.

I didn't travel along the coast very often, but I enjoyed the drive when I did. Anticipating a run-in with Lavender had me gripping the steering wheel tighter than normal.

"Any sign of Cora?" Shawna asked. She sat in the passenger seat, staring out the window and balancing the rubber-banded stack of Nadine's flyers on her lap.

"No," I said, lifting my foot off the accelerator and flipping on the right turn signal.

As I turned onto Treasure Lane, the Beaumont Inn came into view. It was a beautiful two-story building with a rocky coastline and the ocean as a backdrop. The place was one of the oldest well-maintained structures in the area and had a lot of history.

A partial wraparound porch beneath a shingled awning

ran along the front and one side of the exterior. The plant beds were well taken care of, the shrubbery neatly manicured.

The Abbotts were familiar with my vehicle. When I pulled into the parking lot, I drove past several empty spaces and found a spot that wasn't too close to the main entrance. My plan was to get in and out before Lavender discovered that I was in the building. I wasn't afraid of confrontation as much as I was about the topic she'd use to embarrass me.

"Planning for a quick getaway," Shawna asked as she got out of the car.

"You're the one who's always telling me to be prepared for anything," I said, then followed her along the paved sidewalk.

Once inside, I scanned the reception area and spotted Molly working behind the long counter that served as the reservation desk. She was helping an older couple but lifted her head long enough to wave. Her wavy dark brown hair enhanced her rounded cheeks, and the smile she flashed us formed dimples.

The spacious room had large picture windows facing the ocean, a perk for anyone who worked there. The hardwood floor was stained a medium brown and looked like it had been recently polished. A decorative rug covered the space in front of several light tan cushioned chairs sitting next to the wall near the door.

"Hey, Molly," Shawna said as soon as the couple picked up their suitcases and headed for the elevator in the hallway to the left.

"Hey, guys. What can I do for you?" Molly asked cheerfully. "Are you here for an event?"

The inn had some rather nice banquet rooms that they rented out for gatherings and meetings. The last time my friends and I had been there, we'd been working on a committee.

"No," I said. "Nothing like that."

Shawna placed the stack of flyers on the counter. "The police are letting Nadine open The Booty Bazaar tomorrow, and we were hoping you wouldn't mind handing these out to your guests."

The businesses in town looked out for each other, mostly anyway. If the flyers had been for my family's shop, they might accidentally end up in the trash. I figured they'd be safe since Lavender didn't have a problem with Nadine.

"Absolutely," Molly said. "The last batch Nadine dropped off disappeared fairly quickly. Quite a few of the guests mentioned stopping by and seeing what she had for sale." Her expression sobered, and her smile faded. Her gaze lost focus as if she were recalling the details of an unpleasant memory.

"Molly," I said. "Are you okay?"

She snapped to attention. "I was thinking about that nice guy who died."

"What about him?" I asked, trying to sound casual and not too curious.

"He didn't seem at all happy about the sale."

"Oh," I said.

"After I showed him a flyer, he grumbled something I couldn't understand, then stormed out the door," Molly said. "That was the last time I saw him." She blinked away the moisture building in her dark eyes.

"I'm sorry," Shawna said.

"Oh, my gosh." Molly placed her hand on the counter. "I'm the one who should be saying I'm sorry. I forgot you're the one who found him. That must have been awful."

It was, but I didn't want to relive the experience by describing it vocally.

"And quite the coincidence," Lavender said as she came around the corner and stepped behind the counter with Molly. "Seems like you're always around when there's a death in town." She smirked. "One would think you had magical powers."

"Careful, Lavender," I said. "Shawna's wanted me to turn someone into a frog for years. Would you like to volunteer as a test subject?"

Her gaze went wild, and she gasped, then took a cautionary step backward. "You wouldn't dare."

My gifts could be classified as paranormal, but they'd never reach the magical level of someone who could cast spells. "I might if I actually had any powers," I said, winking at Molly, who knew nothing about my spirit-summoning abilities. To her, I was an ordinary person, and I planned to keep it that way, at least for now.

Lavender was big on retribution, so I couldn't blame Molly for placing her hand over her mouth to keep from laughing. Lavender shot a reprimanding glare at her employee anyway, then said, "I'll be in my office if you need me."

I was about to suggest we leave when Shawna tugged my sleeve and tipped her head toward the window. Aaron was standing outside chatting with another man, their conversation looked a bit heated. The man's brown hair was neatly styled in a short layer cut. His attire leaned toward business casual.

"Molly, do you know who those guys are?" Shawna asked, hitching her thumb toward the men. She must've had an ulterior reason for pretending not to know Aaron, so I played along.

I wished I could pinpoint the reason seeing Aaron made me uneasy. Maybe it was because he'd snubbed the town, and I was still experiencing a residual emotional reaction. Whatever the cause, I was interested to know what the two men were discussing. It was too bad Cora hadn't come with us. I would've asked her to eavesdrop.

"The one on the left is Aaron Mercer," Molly said. "He's the appraiser from Portland that's here to help Nadine. The other guy is his boss, Nathan Hansley."

"Hildie's cousin?" Shawna asked.

Molly nodded. "Yeah."

I wondered if Nadine knew he was in town. Had he been here all week? Could he be the person who broke into her shop? Or possibly the person who killed Liam? I couldn't come up with a reasonable explanation for either of those things that made sense. "Do you know when he arrived?" I asked.

"I wasn't here," she said. "But I believe he checked in last night."

"Does he stay here frequently?" I asked.

"Only a couple of times that I know of since Hildie's incident," Molly said, sadness lacing her voice. Maybe she'd known the woman better than I had and was disappointed about the way things turned out. "I think he was checking on her store." She rubbed her chin. "Before that, he was a regular guest and stayed with us at least once a month."

"I didn't realize Hildie and her cousin were that close." If Nathan was making regular trips, why wasn't he staying at her place? If I lived somewhere else and was visiting my family, they'd insist I save my money and room with them.

"I don't know if they were or not," Molly said. "Nathan sometimes met with Jake Durant when he came to town." She sighed. "Before Jake, you know, ended up dead."

That bit of news was informative. I wanted to ask Molly more questions, but movement outside caught my attention. Aaron and Nathan had finished talking and would reach the front of the building in no time. Since Aaron would no doubt recognize Shawna and me, I didn't want to be here when they came inside. "Thanks for all your help, Molly, but we should get going."

"Okay, see you later," Molly said.

I didn't have time for explanations, so I grabbed Shawna's hand and pulled her toward the exit. I didn't let go until we'd reached my car.

If Aaron and Nathan had seen us scurrying across the lot, they didn't stop to comment. "Well, that was interesting," Shawna said, snapping the safety belt across her chest.

I did the same, then pulled the phone out of my purse.

"Who are you calling?" she asked.

I swiped the screen and started typing. "I'm sending Nadine a text to see if she was expecting Nathan."

"Do you think he's here on a nefarious mission?"

"I don't know. If Molly was right about him meeting Jake before he died, then I think it's worth finding out." I hit the send button, then handed Shawna my phone since I didn't want to wait in the parking lot for Nadine to respond. "Let me know what she says."

CHAPTER FIFTEEN

On the way back from the inn, I dropped Shawna at her place before heading to the shop. There were several customers perusing shelves. Jade was standing behind the counter handing out change. Grams was helping a mother and her three boys, their ages in the five to the ten-year-old range, select toys from our pirate section.

"Thank you," the man said to Jade, then smiled at me before picking up his bag and making his way to the door.

"Hey," Jade said. "How was the trip?"

"I'll tell you about it later." We'd been friends long enough that providing a reason wasn't necessary.

"I wasn't sure when you'd get back, so I grabbed you a sandwich," Jade said. "It's in the refrigerator." We had a small employee lunch room in the back, complete with a dinette set and microwave. There was also a coffee maker, which I occasionally used, though my preference was a flavored brew from Mattie's place.

I'd been so preoccupied pondering the information Molly had provided about Nathan that I hadn't realized how close it was to the lunch hour. "Thanks, you're awesome."

"Oh," Jade said, reaching under the counter and

retrieving a sealed cardboard box. "This came while you were out."

I hadn't placed any orders recently, so I wasn't expecting any deliveries. Curious, I read the label and found the sender's name, Parasleuth, Inc. Then, because I had a hard time believing what I was seeing, I read it again.

Jade nudged me with her elbow. "Aren't you going to open it?"

"Yes," I said in an annoyed don't-rush-me tone. My body tingled with anticipation. Surely, if I'd been rejected, they'd have sent a letter, not a package.

Now that I was going to get my long-awaited answer, I was worried about what I'd find inside. "Maybe I should open it in the back."

"Good idea," Jade said. "I'll go with you." She waved her hand to get Gram's attention, then signaled that we'd be in the office.

Jade cleared a spot in the middle of my desk so I'd have a place to set the box. She pulled a pair of scissors out of a drawer and handed them to me. She seemed as nervous as I was, though her reaction was excitement based. Mine was more from fear of the unknown and knowing that opening the package would change the direction of my future.

After taking a deep breath, I cut along the tape seam securing the top. I pushed back the cardboard flaps to reveal a large package that almost filled the inside of the box. It wasn't like any standard mail packet I'd ever seen before. This one was white with a black, ornate design running along the outside border.

Printed in fancy script along the center of the package were the words "*Only to be opened by Rylee Spencer.*"

"That's an unusual design," Jade said, touching the swirls. Sparks erupted underneath her fingertips. "Ouch." She jerked her hand away.

"What did you do?" I asked.

"Nothing. It shocked me," Jade said, then shook her hand as if it still tingled. "I think you should try."

"And maybe I shouldn't." I cringed as memories of the spirit seeker's blue tendrils flashed through my mind. I didn't think being cautious made me a coward.

Jade wiggled her finger at the package. "It has your name on it. Maybe it's magically encoded, so only you can open it."

There was a time when I would've argued with her reasoning. Now I knew anything was possible and believed she might be right.

"Okay," I said, running my sweaty palms along the front of my pants, then hovering my hand inches from the packet's surface. "But if something goes wrong, I'm blaming Shawna since this was her idea." Jade was just as guilty since she'd assisted with the coercion, but Shawna was the main instigator.

She giggled. "Works for me."

I poked the package, expecting a jolt, and was relieved when nothing happened. "Huh," I said as I removed it from the box. "Guess you were right."

"It helps to have a brother with a lot of paranormal experience," Jade said, snatching the empty box out of the way and setting it on the floor near the wall.

"That's for sure," I said, thankful for all the help Bryce had given me in the past.

I used the convenient tab located on one end of the package to get it open, then pulled out the contents; a letter with a similar script to the wording on the packet, a stack of papers thick enough to be a manuscript, and a padded envelope with the return address for Parasleuth, Inc.

The letterhead contained the organization's name printed in black and underlaid in gold. Behind that was an image of a whimsical sheet ghost, its hands touching the top of the letters. It was eye-catching and professional.

"What does it say?" Jade asked, moving to read over my shoulder.

I held up the paper and started reading.

Dear Ms. Spencer,

Thank you for your interest in our Spirit Sleuther Certification. After reviewing your application, we are pleased to inform you that you have qualified for acceptance into our program.

Enclosed you will find a questionnaire that will assist us in matching you with a compatible mentor. Please answer all the questions truthfully and send the document in the enclosed envelope to us as soon as possible.

Sincerely,

Gretchen Thatcher
Owner

Jade tapped my arm. "See, I knew you'd get accepted. Now you can think about becoming a professional sleuther."

"Let's see if I can get certified first." I was more interested in obtaining knowledge. I hadn't decided what I'd do once I'd completed the training.

"You'll do fine," Jade said. "I know it."

I grinned, appreciating my friend's support. "This is going to take a while," I said, fanning through the stack of papers. It seemed odd that the organization wanted the questionnaire filled in by hand. With today's technology, submitting the information would've gone a lot faster if I'd been able to do it online.

"No kidding," Jade said. "You should probably let Shawna know. She'll be thrilled to know you've been accepted."

"Good idea." I pulled the cell out of my purse, swiped the screen with my thumb, and started typing a text. "And, just so you know. If there are any questions about the supernatural." Which I was sure there would be. "I'll need you two to help with the answers."

CHAPTER SIXTEEN

Logan had suggested I come by the station after six. That way, Roy would be gone, and no one else would question anything we did. On my trip there, I stopped at a deli and picked up some sandwiches.

Cora wasn't familiar with Cumberpatch, but I was sure she'd be able to find the police station eventually. I didn't need to worry because she showed up in my apartment right when I was getting ready to leave.

Cora had on the outfit she'd worn the day I met her, but her hair was down and styled in wavy curls. She'd been quiet most of the trip, so after pulling into the lot and parking, I asked, "Are you okay?"

"Yes," she said. "I guess I'm a little nervous and excited."

I understood how she felt. I was apprehensive myself. So many things could go wrong with summoning Liam, and I didn't want to let Cora down. Even more worrisome was my relationship with Logan. The parameters were about to change, and hopefully not in a negative way.

"Come on," I said, grabbing mine and Logan's dinner before getting out of the car. "I'm sure everything will be fine."

Inside, Anthony was working away on the computer behind the counter.

"Hey," I said. "Don't they ever let you go home?"

"Once in a while." He chuckled. "I'll call Logan and let them know you're here."

"Thanks." I took a seat on the bench. It was good that I didn't have to wait long because Cora's pacing wasn't helping my anxiety any.

"Right on time," Logan said, holding out his hand. "Here, let me take that for you." After handing him the bag, I followed him down the hallway.

I was right about the place being lightly staffed this time of the evening. The desks sitting in the middle area were unoccupied. Roy's door was closed, and what I could see of his office through the glass pane on the wall was dark.

We stopped by the drink machine, and he purchased a can of soda for each of us.

The place was pretty quiet, but it didn't stop Logan from glancing around to make sure we were alone before he asked, "Did Cora come with you?"

"Yes," I said, glancing toward my other side where she was walking next to me.

Logan couldn't see Cora, but if he paid close attention to the cold surrounding her body, he could determine her approximate location. After I entered his office, he held the door open longer than necessary to give Cora time to enter.

"Your detective has wonderful manners," Cora said as she swept into the room.

Even I found his courteous behavior endearing. "Cora says thank you."

"You're most welcome," Logan said.

"Cora, do you mind if we eat first?" I asked. I knew I was stalling, but I preferred having a full stomach before dealing with the Liam situation. Not that being zapped drained my energy. It was just an unpleasant experience.

"No," she said. "Please, go ahead."

Once Logan and I were seated, me in one of the guest chairs and him behind the desk, I pulled the sandwiches out of the bag and placed one in front of each of us. We spent the next few minutes enjoying our meal.

"How did your trip to the inn go?" he asked.

"I offered to turn Lavender into a frog," I said.

Logan coughed, nearly choking on the bite he'd taken. He swallowed some of his drink, then said, "Did you acquire a new superpower you forgot to mention?"

I rolled my eyes. "No."

"Did you learn anything interesting?" Logan asked.

"I did." I set my half-eaten sandwich back on the wrapper I was using as a plate. "I know you're a stickler for the rules, and I don't want you to do anything that would put your job at risk. Before I share the information, I need to know what this collaboration of yours entails." My mother and grandmother were both expert negotiators and had taught me well. I had a ghost to save, and boyfriend or not, Cora's afterlife future was a priority.

Logan reached across the desk and placed his hand over mine. "I realize summoning another spirit is a big deal and will cause you additional stress. I want you to know that I trust you, and I'm willing to share everything I've learned regarding Liam's case."

"Does that include anything you found out about Cora as well?" I asked. There was no way he hadn't already done some digging into what happened to her.

He chuckled and retrieved his hand. "Of course."

"Great, what did you find out?" I asked.

"Fair enough, I'll go first," he said, giving me a pass on sidestepping his question. "I spoke with someone from the police department in Brindburrow, and they think Cora's death was the result of interrupting a burglary, not something premeditated."

Hearing her death hadn't been planned didn't make me feel much better. "Did they ever find out who broke into her home?" Since she was still around, and I believed the thief and her killer were the same person, I had a feeling I already knew the answer. Maybe Logan had learned something useful.

Logan shook his head. "No, it looked like a professional job. Nothing was ransacked. They assumed the thief knew what they were looking for, which happened to be her deceased husband's antique weapon collection and some of Cora's jewelry."

I glanced at Cora to see if there was anything else she wanted to add. She shook her head. "That ties to what she remembers."

"It explains how her brooch left her home but not how it ended up in Nadine's shop," Logan said. "Back to you and your visit."

I flashed him a wry grin. "Did you know that Hildie's cousin Nathan who lives in Portland is currently staying at the inn and used to make regular trips to town?"

Logan washed the last bite of his sandwich down with his drink. "Should I have?"

"Probably not," I said. "Apparently, on some of those trips, maybe even all of them, he met with Jake Durant."

"Really. That *is* interesting," he said, leaning back in his chair.

"I thought so too." I crumpled up our empty sandwich wrappers, stuffed them back in the bag, then handed it to Logan so he could deposit it in the trashcan in the corner behind his desk.

"I don't suppose you were able to find out how long he's been in town?"

Logan's suspicious thoughts seemed to follow the same path as mine. "He arrived yesterday, but I thought it was strange that Nadine didn't even know he was coming." A fact she'd confirmed when she responded to my text.

"Do I want to know how you discovered the information?" he asked, his tone insinuating that I'd been doing something I shouldn't have at the time.

"I saw him from the reception area. Shawna was with me and saw him too."

Logan snorted, letting me know he thought my friend's reliability was questionable. I couldn't blame him after her conspiratorial stunt at his crime scene.

"And," I said. "We saw him arguing with Aaron Mercer, the appraiser helping Nadine." Not that disagreements between colleagues were uncommon.

"Did you overhear what they were discussing?" Logan asked.

"No, but maybe you should talk to both of them."

"I already spoke with Aaron, and everyone else Nadine said had been helping her prior to Liam's death."

"And…" I said.

"And nothing," Logan sighed. "Other than being unpleasant, Aaron wasn't helpful."

I thought the man was rude, but maybe he was nicer to Logan because he worked for law enforcement.

"The rest had no idea why someone would want to break into Nadine's place."

Neither did I, at least not anyone local. "Can you question Nathan to see if he knows anything?"

Logan massaged the back of his neck. "I can't make accusations or interrogate anyone without something substantial to go on. Right now, I've got nothing. No witnesses. And a bunch of fingerprints that most likely came from customers. Whoever committed the crime must've worn gloves because there wasn't anything on the dagger's hilt."

"Which is why you wanted my help," I said.

"Pretty much," he said. "I'm convinced Cora's death is somehow linked to what happened to Liam. I need something that will help me prove it."

"We already know Hildie was tangled up with Jake. If Nathan was too, it might be a connection worth checking, don't you think?"

"I do," Logan said. "And I'll look into it after we're

finished here."

"Well then." I pushed out of my chair. "I think we should get after it."

"Me too," Cora said as she slid off the lateral filing cabinet where she'd been sitting. She hadn't said a word during our conversation, and I'd almost forgotten she was in the room with us.

Logan lifted a dark blue suitcase off the floor and placed it on its side on his desk. After unzipping the top, he asked, "What do you think would work the best?"

"What's in there?" I asked, pointing at a small brown leather travel case tucked in the corner next to some folded shirts. The letters "LE" were embossed in gold on one of the corners.

Logan unzipped the case and lifted the lid. Inside was a cylindrical toothbrush container, a razor, a travel-size bottle of shampoo, and another containing conditioner. There was also some men's cologne.

"Let's go with the toothbrush." I didn't think we could get any more personal than that.

"Okay," Logan said, pulling off the plastic cap to expose the brush.

"Here we go," I said, then silently chanted, "Please let it be Liam" over and over in my mind.

As soon as I wrapped my fingers around the toothbrush, a jolt, much stronger than the one I'd felt when I'd touched Cora's brooch, spread from my palm to my elbow. It was also more painful than usual, and I instinctively flung it into the suitcase.

"I think the summoning part worked." I shook my hand and wiggled my fingers, trying to erase the sensation. The pain had faded, but the tingling remained.

Logan furrowed his brows and placed his hands on my arms. "You look a little pale. Are you all right? Do you need to sit down?"

"I'm fine," I said, placing my palm on his cheek. "I promise."

"Is it always like this?" he asked.

"It's different every time, but yes."

"Rylee," Cora said, wringing her hands together. "If I'd known it caused you pain, I never would have asked you to do it."

"Cora, it's okay," I said. "It's like being shocked and doesn't last very long." Which was the truth because the tingling was already subsiding.

"How long do we have to wait before someone appears?" Logan asked.

"It varies," I said. "Hopefully, not much longer." The air immediately chilled as if my words possessed their own magic and had called to the spirit. A form took shape near the door and quickly manifested into Liam.

Since he was a new spirit, his body shimmered a translucent blue brighter than Cora's. Besides being a ghost, he wore the same clothes and looked exactly the way he had the morning I'd seen him at Nadine's place.

"Is it him?" Logan asked.

"Uh-huh," I said, relieved that I'd only called one ghost and it had been the right one.

"Liam," Cora said, her voice crackling.

"Grandma," Liam said. "What are you doing here? I thought you were…gone." He pulled her into a tight hug and held onto her for the longest time.

I didn't understand all the rules governing the spirit world. When humans and ghosts interacted, they passed through one another. Apparently, ghosts could see and touch each other the same way humans did. I glimpsed the back of his jacket, glad I didn't see any evidence of his stabbing.

"Liam, sweetie," Cora said in a soothing tone normally used on children. "I'm afraid you died, and you're a ghost like me."

"No, that can't be." Liam groaned and slumped against the wall. Cora grabbed his hand to keep him from disappearing into the adjoining office.

His misery was upsetting, and I tried to offer some encouragement. "I'm Rylee, and this is my boyfriend Logan, who is also a police detective. We want to help you find out what happened."

Liam straightened, then pointed at me. "I've seen you before, but I can't remember where." He rubbed his forehead. "Actually, I can remember things that happened weeks ago, but anything recent seems a bit fuzzy."

"I'm afraid the memory issue comes with being a new spirit," I said. "It may take a little time for you to remember what happened."

"How long?" Liam asked.

"Everyone is different." I still believed he held an important clue to solving Cora's murder as well as his own. So, in Liam's case, I hoped his recall happened sooner rather than later.

I'd made sure to include enough details with my side of the conversation for Logan to follow.

"What do we do now?" Logan asked.

"We give Liam a little time to acclimate." In other words, we avoided pressuring him for answers.

"Since his memories haven't returned yet, do you mind if I spend some time alone with Liam?" Cora asked.

"There isn't much more we can do tonight, so I think spending time together is a good idea," I said. "Can you meet me at the shop in the morning?"

"Yes," Cora said, then took Liam's hand, causing them both to disappear.

"Are they gone?" Logan asked.

"Yes," I said, slipping on my jacket and reaching for my purse. "I should go too so you can get back to work." I also needed to call Shawna and Jade to let them know summoning Liam had been a success. I knew he'd have problems with his memory, but I was disappointed that we hadn't made any headway with his case.

"Thank you." Logan stepped in front of me and placed his hands on my hips. "Your spirit sleuther skills are greatly appreciated."

"You're welcome." I placed my hands on his chest, the mention of sleuthing reminding me about the package I'd received earlier. "I almost forgot to tell you. I've officially been approved for the certification program."

"That's great." He grinned. "When do you start?"

"I'm not sure. I have to fill out and send back their questionnaire. Then they'll assign me a mentor." I went on to tell him how the package had zapped Jade but hadn't affected me.

"That's a serious safety measure," he said. "Did you get a chance to look at any of the questions?"

"Not yet," I said. "I've kind of been busy helping my boyfriend solve some crimes."

"Sounds like a lucky guy to me," he said, pressing his lips to mine and giving me a kiss that made me forget all about ghosts and murder.

CHAPTER SEVENTEEN

Nadine called me shortly after I'd arrived at work in the morning and told me she'd found something interesting. Something she wanted to show me rather than explain over the phone. My first impulse was to rush to her place, but Cora and Liam had agreed to meet me at my family's shop, and I needed to be there when they appeared. We hadn't set a specific time, so I kept myself busy catching up on the paperwork stacked on my desk, then going up front to help with customers.

Time passed quickly, and it was midafternoon by the time the flow of shoppers had diminished, and Grams, Jade, and I had a chance to take a break. Which also happened to be around the same time Shawna strolled into the store. After working the lunch shift at the restaurant, the aroma of cooked foods still clung to her uniform.

"Hey, everyone." She laid a newspaper on the counter by the cash register, then turned to me. "Did you tell Grams what we learned about Nathan yesterday?"

"She filled me in before we opened," Grams answered for me.

"Do you think he's connected to what happened at Nadine's place?" Jade asked.

"I don't know, but Logan seemed interested after I told him, so he's going to do some additional investigating."

"How about Liam?" Shawna asked. "Was he able to remember anything?"

I sighed. "I haven't seen him or Cora yet." I was starting to get a little worried and had to remind myself that ghosts couldn't carry around cell phones or wear wristwatches to help them tell time.

"Feels like we're getting visitors," Grams said, rubbing her arms.

I noticed the chill right before Liam and Cora appeared in the middle of the aisle. They each wore a brightly colored T-shirt, khaki shorts that reached the top of their knees, and tennis shoes. I had no idea why they'd chosen to dress like tourists and struggled to keep the amusement out of my voice when I said their names.

This was the second time after wishing I'd see Cora that she'd appeared. I planned to ask my mentor, when I was finally assigned one, if my abilities could be controlled by my thoughts.

"I'm sorry we're late," Cora said.

"It's okay," I said. Where they went and what they did was their business. Unless it involved scaring the locals and ended up in the newspaper, I didn't need to know.

"I was fascinated by our visit with Edith and Joyce, so I took Liam to see the Classic Broom."

"That place is quite unusual," Liam said. My interaction with him had been limited, so I couldn't tell if he was being sarcastic or had truly been impressed with the Haverstons's store.

"Now that you're here," I said. "I was hoping you wouldn't mind going to Nadine's shop with me." I spoke directly to Liam. "I'll understand if you don't want to go." If I was a ghost, I wasn't sure how I'd feel about visiting the place where I died.

"Do you think it will help with my memories?" Liam asked.

"It's possible." I tried to sound positive without giving him false expectations. "Even if what you remember is vague, the tiniest detail could be important."

Cora placed a comforting hand on his arm. "I think we should go."

Liam smiled at his grandmother. "So do I."

***

Fifteen minutes later, and after calling Nadine to let her know we were coming, Cora, Liam, and I entered The Booty Bazaar. The place looked a lot different than it had a few days ago. The broken glass on the front door had been replaced. A lot of the items were gone, and some of the shelves were bare.

The delivery company she'd hired must've sent a truck because most of the larger pieces of furniture had been removed, creating a more spacious look in the middle of the shop. People were milling around, but not as many as there'd been on opening day. At the rate things were selling, Nadine would be able to start renovations in a couple of days.

I moved farther into the room, noting that Nadine had placed a throw rug over the area where Liam's blood had stained the floor. I shot a sidelong glance at Liam to see if he had noticed. His brows were furrowed, and he was slowly pacing around the room, no doubt trying to remember something. Cora stood to the side, silently watching him, her expression filled with concern and caring. Coming here seemed to be hard on both of them.

"Good morning, Rylee. I'll be with you in a minute," Nadine said, then went back to assisting a middle-aged woman who muttered something about having difficulty making a decision.

After responding with a smile, I observed a china set sitting on a shelf a few feet away. I wasn't interested in purchasing the dishes but needed something to keep me busy and aid with calming the anxiety surging through my system.

Apparently, it wasn't working because I jumped when Nadine approached me from behind a little later.

"Sorry," she said.

"Given my, um,"—I lowered my voice—"ability, you'd think I was immune to being startled."

"Come on." She motioned me toward the back of the room. "I'll show you what I found." Before entering the hallway, she called, "Ben."

"Over here," he said as he popped up from behind a nearby display case where he'd been rearranging items on the shelf. He saw me and smiled. "Hey, Rylee."

"How's it going?" I asked.

"Busy…and interesting." He spoke to Nadine. "Did you need me to do something?"

"Rylee and I are going in back for a few minutes," Nadine said. "Can you keep an eye on things while I'm gone?"

"Sure. No problem."

"We'll stay out here and keep looking around," Cora said.

"Maybe I'll remember something while you're gone," Liam added.

I couldn't answer without drawing unwanted attention from customers, so I gave them a brief nod.

"No Aaron today," I asked as I followed Nadine to her office.

"Nathan contacted me not long after you did yesterday to let me know he was in town and planned to stop by the shop today." She pulled a key out of her pants pocket and unlocked the door. "He and Aaron went to grab a coffee and should be back shortly."

At least Nathan had been forthcoming about being in town. "When Shawna and I stopped by the inn, we saw Nathan and Aaron arguing about something." I hadn't mentioned what we'd seen at the inn when I sent her a text. "Any idea what it was about?"

"Not a clue. Other than letting Aaron know Logan had released the crime scene, we haven't discussed much. Nathan showed up late, and I was busy, so we haven't had an opportunity to talk."

"Does Nathan still have the code for the back door?" I'd already confirmed with Molly that he hadn't been staying at the inn when Liam was killed, but that didn't mean he wasn't in town. Was it possible he used the alley door to get into the shop, then broke the window to make it look like a burglary?

"Yes," Nadine said. "I meant to change it, but things got busy with the opening, and I didn't have a chance." She frowned. "Why?"

"Not any specific reason. Just speculating."

"Okay." Nadine didn't sound convinced, but she didn't press me to explain.

"I brought Cora and Liam with me," I said once we were safely inside with the door closed.

"Abby told me the summoning was a success." She glanced around. "Are they here with us now?"

"No, they'd stayed up front," I said. "Liam is hoping he might remember something."

"It must be awful for him to see where he was murdered." Nadine moved around her desk and sat in front of her computer.

Even more so after he'd regained his memory and had to relive what happened. "I don't think it's easy for Cora either, but at least they're getting to spend time together." Which would hopefully last once they moved on to their afterlife.

She opened the ledger and placed it to the left of her keyboard. "None of the items listed here got logged into the computer inventory."

"It sounds like our theory about Hildie purposely excluding items from her inventory was correct." I stepped behind the desk to look at the monitor with her.

"Yes, but here's the interesting part. I went through all the travel expenses and purchases logged in the computer and compared them with the dates in the ledger. The trips coinciding with these purchases,"—Nadine tapped the open page in the ledger—"were all made to Portland."

"Did she make any trips to Brindburrow?"

"Not that I could find," Nadine said. "But I did a map search online and discovered that Brindburrow is less than an hour's drive from Portland."

I moved to the other side of the room and started pacing, trying to organize the clues we'd gathered so far. "We know the dagger on your flyer belonged to Cora and was stolen, along with other items. So maybe the thief sold it to Hildie directly or worked through another party."

"Do you think it was someone who worked for Jake?" Nadine asked.

"Possibly." Since Hildie was in jail, I couldn't ask her. Not that I thought she'd willingly want to help me.

"We still need to figure out how Liam knew the dagger was in Cumberpatch," I said.

"Which won't happen until he regains his memory," Nadine said.

"Yeah." When I turned to start pacing again, I noticed a green glow coming from a box sitting on the floor in the corner.

"What's in there?" I asked, pointing.

Nadine picked up the box and set it on the edge of her desk. "I found this in the lower cabinet compartment of an antique armoire when the movers came to load the furniture." She pushed back the cardboard flaps. "There was a small chest blocking the doors, so I don't think anyone realized this was in there."

"Didn't Nathan do an inventory before selling you the store?"

Not that discrepancies didn't happen. When my family and I did our annual inventory, we always had product balances that weren't accurate, something that often occurred in the retail business.

"He said he did and also provided me with a printout." Nadine reached into the box, pulled out a crystal ball, and set it on the desk.

The globe was the size of a bowling ball and sat on a bronze base comprised of four legs, each sculpted into the shape of a dragon-like serpent. "Is it supposed to glow like that?" I asked. I'd only gotten a glimpse of the one Nadine had at her old shop and remembered it being made of clear glass.

Nadine's gaze jumped from me to the ball. "Glow?"

"Yes," I said. "There's a swirly mist inside the ball."

"I don't see anything," Nadine said. "Do you think there may be magic attached to it?" She leaned forward to get a better look.

Nadine had supernatural gifts of her own. Since she'd already touched the ball, and nothing happened, I was fairly certain the magic didn't affect her. I couldn't be sure about myself, so I took a step back, determined to avoid all contact. The moving smoke was almost mesmerizing, and I had trouble looking away.

The longer I stared at the crystal ball, the more I thought about Edith and her prediction. *A discovery from the past will bring clarity to the future.* Of course, I still had no clue what she'd meant or why her words picked this moment to pop into my mind.

Solving the mysteries of the mystical globe would have to wait for a later date. "What else is in the box?" I asked.

"Take a look at this." She reached inside, pulled out a short sword that looked old and authentic, then tried to hand it to me.

"I'd rather not," I said, waving her away.

"Sorry," she said after realizing why I was hesitant to examine the contents.

"Rylee," Cora said as she burst from the wall, skimming my shoulder and causing goosebumps to form along my arm. Liam sailed into the room a few seconds later, his frantic expression mirroring his grandmother's.

"Cora, Liam, what's wrong?" I asked.

"That man out there." Cora shook her hand at the closed door. "I've seen him before."

"What man?" I asked.

"The one who appraised Archie's antique weapons," Cora said.

"His name is Aaron Mercer. Are you saying he's the one who authenticated your husband's weapons?" I asked, cluing Nadine into our conversation.

"Yes." Cora's gaze dropped to the sword Nadine was holding. "Where did you find that? It belonged to Archie…well, Liam now."

"Are you sure?" I asked.

"Yes, I'm sure," she huffed. "Archie spent hours taking care of his collection."

Liam looked inside the box. "She's right. The cutlass and flintlock pistol were also his."

"These items belonged to Cora's husband," I said to Nadine.

"That's… I want to say interesting, but it's disappointing and upsetting," Nadine said. "And makes me wonder how many other stolen items found their way into the shop."

Had Liam inadvertently stumbled across a theft ring? It wouldn't be the first one to find its way to Cumberpatch.

I'd been so focused on Nathan and his connection to Jake that I hadn't considered Aaron as a possible suspect. Without any proof, I couldn't prove whether it was Nathan or Aaron who'd killed Cora and Liam. Or if it was both.

I couldn't stop thinking about the crystal ball or the word "clarity" from Edith's prediction. Things started to make sense, and before I could rationalize the dangers involved in what I was about to do, I blurted out, "I have a plan. Follow my lead."

CHAPTER EIGHTEEN

When Nadine and I returned to the shop, Ben, Aaron, and Nathan were the only people left in the building. Cora and Liam had followed behind us, then found a place in the center of the room where they'd have an unobstructed view of everything that was about to take place.

"I'm glad to see you're back," Nadine said as she placed the box containing Archie's weapons on the counter closest to Aaron and Nathan. We'd agreed that leaving the crystal ball locked in her office should keep it safe until we could figure out what to do with it. "Ben, why don't you call it a day?"

"Are you sure you don't need me to help you close?" Ben's voice held a note of worry.

"No, I can handle it." She smiled. "You've worked hard and done a great job, so please, go have some fun."

"Thanks." He grinned, then grabbed his jacket off a hook on the back wall. "I'll see you tomorrow."

I waited for Ben to disappear out the front door. "Hello, Aaron," I said. "It's nice to see you again." My cordial tone was the same one I used when dealing with unpleasant customers.

Ignoring his grumbled greeting, I smiled at Nathan.

Since we'd never officially met, I acted like I didn't know who he was. "Hi, I'm Rylee." I held out my hand.

"Nathan," he said, finishing the gesture.

"Oh, you're Hildie Simpkins cousin." Bringing up his jailbird relative wasn't going to earn me any friendship points. Not that being associated with the man was important. By the time our conversation ended, I expected to be one of his least favorite people.

"That's right," he said, clenching his fist against his thigh.

I'd touched a nerve and deliberated whether or not mentioning Jake would be a good idea. I decided to save that tidbit for later if I didn't get the reaction I was looking for with the rest of our discussion.

I shifted sideways to nonchalantly glimpse the other half of the room and make sure Liam and Cora were still with us. The way Liam kept staring at the rug covering the floor, I wondered if his memories were starting to return. I'd have to wait until after Aaron and Nathan left before asking him what he remembered.

"Nadine found a box of stuff hidden in one of the armoires," I said, cuing her with a glance.

She lifted the flaps. "Aaron, would you mind looking at these items to see if they're worth anything?"

"Yes, of course," he said. "It would be my pleasure."

"Great," Nadine said. She reached into the box and carefully retrieved the cutlass, pistol, and short sword, placing them side-by-side on the counter.

I'd been paying close attention to Aaron's face and noticed a glimmer of recognition before he picked up the cutlass and examined it, then moved on to the other two items. When he was finished, he gave Nadine a weak smile. "They're certainly old and quite valuable."

"That's the same thing he told Archie," Cora said.

It was too bad she was a ghost. She would've made a great witness.

It was time for me to implement my plan. I pointed at

the sword and said, "That piece has a hilt similar to the dagger the guy who died was looking for." I walked over, grabbed a sales flyer off the stack near the cash register, then slapped it on the counter next to Aaron. "See."

The hilts didn't look anything alike, but I'd shocked Aaron into widening his dark eyes. Before either man could comment, I pulled out my cell phone, then pretended to swipe the screen and access a number.

"Wait," Aaron growled. "What are you doing?"

"I think we should report our findings to Detective Prescott." I held up a finger to cut him off, then placed the phone next to my ear. "Hey, Logan, it's Rylee," I said to my imaginary boyfriend. "Nadine found some antique weapons that we believe belonged to your murder victim."

I took a few steps away, bobbing my head as if listening to something important. "Oh, okay." I paused again. "I'll be sure to tell her." I faked another swipe to end the call and stuffed the phone back in my pocket. "Logan definitely wants to see what you found, but he won't be able to stop by until tomorrow morning. He suggested you secure the items in your office."

"I can do that," Nadine said, picking up the weapons and returning them to the box.

Nathan's gaze was focused on the box as he spoke. "We can stick around and help you lock up."

"That's really thoughtful of you guys," I said. "But I already volunteered to help." There was no way I was leaving Nadine alone with either of them.

"Well then, I guess we should go," Nathan said. Aaron looked like he wanted to argue, but Nathan stopped him by motioning him toward the door.

It seemed Nadine didn't want to give them a chance to change their minds. She hurried to engage the lock and flip the sign to "Closed." She slumped with her back against the door and blew out a relieved breath. "That went well, don't you think?"

I was doing some heavy breathing myself, trying to get

my accelerated heartbeat to slow down. "I do." I wasn't an actress, but I was certain if Shawna and Jade had been there, they'd commend me on my performance.

"Yes, I agree," Cora said. "That was most impressive."

"Liam, are you all right?" I asked. He hadn't moved and was staring at the back of the shop again.

He jerked his gaze to the rest of us and said, "I remember what happened."

"You do?" I asked excitedly. "Will it bother you to share the details?"

Equally interested, Nadine pushed away from the door as if standing next to me would help her hear what Liam had to say.

"No," he said. "Someone slipped a note under the door of my room at the inn."

"What did the note say?" I asked.

"If I wanted information about my dagger, I needed to meet them at this address."

I repeated what he said to Nadine.

"The police didn't find a note." I knew Logan would've mentioned it if he had.

"It was in my pocket, so maybe the killer took it," Liam said.

"Speaking of killers, did you get a look at the person who did this to you?" I asked.

"No," he groaned. "When I arrived, the front door was unlocked, so I came inside. I made it as far as that display case over there." He tucked his arms across his chest. "The last thing I remember was an excruciating pain in my back."

I shared with Nadine, who gasped, then said, "Oh, Liam, I'm so sorry that happened to you...and in my shop."

"Please tell her it's not her fault," Liam said. "I suspected I was dealing with Cora's killer and should've known better than to come inside." He looked lovingly at his grandmother. "But I wanted answers."

Cora sniffled. "I understand."

"Liam's right. You aren't to blame," I said to Nadine. "But if my plan works, we should catch a killer." Maybe two.

"Now, all I have to do is share the details with everybody else." And I could already think of one person who wouldn't be happy that I'd initiated a dangerous situation without discussing it with him first. I retrieved my phone again, and used the speed dial for Logan.

CHAPTER NINETEEN

Jade's shoulder brushed against mine, and she asked in a lowered voice, "Are you sure this is going to work?"

Grams, Shawna, Jade, and I, were all hiding with Nadine in the storage room at the back of her shop. Most of the shelves were empty, but there wasn't anywhere to sit, so we huddled near the closed door.

We couldn't afford to be discovered and had foregone using anything to light the interior. The room was pitch black, and even after my eyes adjusted, the most I could see of my grandmother and friends were their darkened shapes.

Logan, being detective first, boyfriend second, insisted we all wait somewhere safe. He and Roy were hiding in the shop. My parents and Max weren't happy about being omitted from the stakeout. After some heavy-duty insistence by the sheriff, they had agreed to remain at home.

I'd thought about calling Molly to verify that Aaron and Nathan were at the inn, but that would've involved an explanation. One that might easily reach the town's gossip line and ruin my plans. Luckily, I had two ghosts who were more than happy to take on the dual role of scout and lookout.

Since Cora and Liam could travel voluntarily, they'd trailed after Aaron and Nathan to ensure they'd returned to the inn and not hung around near the shop waiting for it to get dark. After checking in, Cora and Liam promised to stay nearby and let me know if Aaron and/or Nathan made an appearance.

For those of us who couldn't walk through walls, getting back into the shop without being seen had been tricky. We didn't want neighboring store owners to see us, so we'd gone into stealth mode, using side streets and entering through the alley entrance. When Roy came up with the plan, none of us told him or Logan that we'd successfully made a similar trip.

"I hope so," I said, trying to sound more confident than I felt. After Liam told Nadine and me that the shop's front door had been unlocked the night he died, I figured either Aaron or Nathan had a key, knew the numerical sequence to the back door, or both. If I was wrong and the front window ended up broken again, I'd gladly pay to have it repaired.

"And, because I'm out of ideas." Cora and Liam were also running out of time. I couldn't narrow the amount they had left to days, hours, or minutes. It was more like a feeling, a sense of urgency, governed by an internal warning that grew stronger the longer it took me to solve their murders.

"At least it's warm, and we're not all crammed together like those little canned fish," Shawna said.

"You mean sardines?" Grams asked.

"Yeah," Shawna said.

"Dead fish aside," Grams said. "I hope we don't have to wait much longer. My bladder will start complaining."

"We haven't even been in here an hour," I said.

Grams tsked. "It never hurts to be prepared."

"Told you," Shawna snickered.

Glaring at my grandmother and frowning at my

giggling friends was a waste of time because none of them could see my face.

Cora's face, however, I could see clearly when her glowing head appeared in the middle of the door. "They're here," she said excitedly, then vanished.

It was a good thing I wasn't a shrieker; otherwise, we'd have been discovered. Though, I did squeak loud enough for Grams to ask, "Rylee, are you okay?"

"Surprise visit from Cora," I whispered. "We have guests."

As if prompted by my announcement, Nathan's voice filtered from the other side of the door. "What do you mean it's not there?"

"Take a look for yourself if you don't believe me," Aaron said.

A thrill raced through my system as I imagined the shocked looks on both their faces. I'd purposely left them with the impression that the box would be in Nadine's office, but it was up front, sitting on the counter. Now that I knew the two men were working together, it was easy to assume what they'd been arguing about when Shawna and I saw them at the inn.

"You don't think the silly woman took it home with her, do you?" Aaron snarled.

"Who's he calling 'silly'?" Nadine whispered. "You or me?"

"No clue," I whispered back.

"I'll check the storeroom," Nathan said. "You look up front."

Creaks on the wooden floor outside the door sent tension pulsing through the small room. Jade wrapped her fingers around my arm in a death grip, her nails digging into my skin. The muscles in my chest tightened, and if I had supernatural hearing, my racing pulse wouldn't be the only one pounding in my ears.

I fumbled to find the lock on the door, engaging it at the same time the handle started to move.

"Found it," Aaron hollered.

As soon as Nathan's footsteps faded, I released the breath I'd been holding. Not long after that, I heard what sounded like scuffling, followed by Roy shouting, "Hold it right there!" I took it as a sign that we could finally escape from our hiding place. The others must've assumed the same thing because they all poured into the hallway with me.

The lights were on when we reached the front of the shop. Aaron and Nathan sat in the middle of the room on chairs from a dinette set. Logan and Roy were standing on either side of them, their stances intimidating.

"Rylee, can you ask which one of them was responsible for taking our lives?" Cora asked, her tone pleading.

Roy didn't know about my ghostly ability. I shook my head the tiniest bit, hoping Cora understood that I couldn't respond directly to her questions. I walked over to Logan and leaned close so I wouldn't be overheard. "I know you'd rather wait to question them at the station, but Cora and Liam are here and need some answers so they can move on."

Everyone else in the room wanted answers as well. Since none of us were police officials, we wouldn't be allowed to be part of the interrogation.

"I'll see what I can do," Logan whispered back.

I moved to stand with my friends, noting Nadine's crossed arms and flushed face. She obviously had other ideas about how the questioning should go and asked, "Would you care to explain what you're doing in *my* shop and how you got inside?" She tapped her foot.

"Starting with the night you broke in and killed Liam Emerson," I said.

"That wasn't me," Nathan said. "It was him. He used the keys and the code I gave him for the back door."

Nadine shot an angered glare at Nathan. "You told me I had all the keys when we signed the sales documents."

Nathan shrugged. "I lied."

"Obviously, but why?" I asked.

When Nathan refused to answer, I said, "We know about your partnership with Jake, so you might as well tell us what you know." It had only been guesswork on my part, but it worked.

"Jake had quite the operation, which ended with his death," Nathan said. "Aaron was supposed to collect any remaining stolen items left in the shop."

"But somehow, Liam found out and ruined your plan, didn't he?" Logan asked.

"I overheard his conversation with Nadine when he came into the shop looking for the dagger," Aaron said. "I was afraid he'd go to the police. When I found out he was staying at the inn, I slipped a note under his door and lured him here."

"We never found any note," Roy said.

"That's because I took it from his pocket and destroyed it." Aaron sneered.

Aaron could act as smug as he wanted. By admitting to taking the note, he'd placed himself at the murder scene. "What about Cora Emerson? Did you stab her in the back as well?"

"The old lady wasn't planned," Aaron said. "She wasn't supposed to be home, and I hadn't meant to hit her so hard."

Cora gasped. Liam snarled and draped his arm around her shoulder. If he was still alive, I had no doubts that Aaron would be on the floor, avoiding punches to his jaw.

"I was afraid she'd recognize me if she caught me with her husband's antique collection," Aaron said. "I didn't want to go to jail."

"Which you're going to be doing anyway," Logan said.

"This is all your fault," Nathan said, clenching his jaw and gritting his teeth so hard I feared they would crack. "If you hadn't killed the woman, I wouldn't be here now trying to clean up your mess."

"If anyone's to blame for this, it's you," Aaron said,

pointing a finger at Nathan. "If you hadn't given Nadine your client addresses, that Liam fellow never would've gotten the flyer."

"The flyer was addressed to Archie," Liam said. "I had all of Cora's mail forwarded to me after she passed away."

Nadine's beautifully designed flyer was the instigating piece that connected everything together.

Now that the killer had been found and their deaths explained, Cora and Liam had no reason to stick around. "Thank you, Rylee," Cora said.

"Yes," Liam said. "We appreciate everything you and your friends did for us." He slowly faded as he took his grandmother's hand, then disappeared completely.

Flashing lights appeared as a police cruiser parked on the street outside. Nadine hurried to unlock the door, so Elliott could rush inside. "Is everyone okay?" he asked. "What did I miss?"

CHAPTER TWENTY

ONE WEEK LATER

Nadine's sale was finally over, and the renovations for her new shop were underway. Another week and she'd officially be relocated and open for business. I didn't know if the crystal ball she'd found posed any dangers. She promised to keep it safely locked away in her storeroom until after I was assigned a mentor and could hopefully obtain some answers.

With that in mind, I spent the night before working on the questionnaire I'd received from Parasleuth, Inc. Even with Jade and Shawna's help during a pizza and wine cooler dinner, it had taken me several hours to complete.

Some of the questions made no sense, like the one asking if there were any witches in my ancestry. Grams was convinced my great-great Uncle Howard occasionally possessed rodents so he could come back to help his relatives. I didn't think that counted and omitted it from my answers.

Rather than give the envelope to the shop's postal person, I decided to take it to the nearest blue metal drop-off box on the other side of the park. The document I clutched to my chest was going to change the direction of my future. I needed to make absolutely sure this was what I wanted. I figured a stroll, some fresh air, and no friends or family to sway me one way or the other would reinforce my decision.

I hadn't seen Cora and Liam since the night they'd disappeared after hearing Aaron confess to their murders, and hoped they'd reunited with Archie.

When I finally reached the box, I gripped the handle and froze. The weather was warm, yet cold air wrapped around me.

"I hope you know you're doing the right thing," Cora said. "There are so many spirits that need someone like you to help them." She swiped at imaginary tears. "Well, you and your wonderful support group."

I'd be the first to admit my family and friends were great, that they'd be there for me no matter what happened. "Thanks. That means a lot."

"You might want to consider opening your own business," Cora said. "I know if I'd been alive when Liam died, I would've paid someone as reputable as you to investigate his death. With all the paranormal enthusiasts living in Cumberpatch, I can't imagine your services wouldn't be welcomed." She smiled. "Should you decide to come out of the ghostly closet, that is."

I laughed. "You might be right, and I promise to give your advice a lot of thought."

"Good." She sniffled again. "It was a pleasure knowing you. Please take care of yourself."

"I will," I said, watching her fade for the final time.

I may not have wanted my gift, but it wasn't going anywhere, and neither was I. Maybe Cora was right, and it was time to step out of the shadows and use my abilities to help others.

With a satisfied grin, I pulled the mailbox door open and dropped the envelope inside.

<<<<>>>>

ABOUT THE AUTHOR

Nola Robertson grew up in the Midwest and eventually migrated to a rural town in New Mexico, where she lives with her husband and three cats, all with unique personalities and a lot of attitude.

Though she started her author career writing paranormal and sci-fi romance, it didn't take long for her love of solving mysteries to have her writing cozies. When she's not busy working on her next DIY project or reading, she's plotting her next mystery adventure.

Made in the USA
Columbia, SC
21 January 2023